She flew in larger and larger circles, looking for anything that might give her a clue as to why her energy felt so off. It wasn't only the human body that sensed it. Things felt off to her Fae self too.

It had been thousands of years since she'd been in this area in her sylph body. The coastlines had changed. The surrounding area had been drained hundreds of years ago.

Yet, the sea appeared to be taking it back. Was it the melting of the polar ice caps? The water would eventually swallow large parts of the U.K.

She could feel an eagerness on the part of the sea. A desire to conquer more land. Skye swooped down close enough to feel the icy spray on her face.

The sea was alive still, even though they'd imprisoned Domnu. Or had they? Was it possible to truly contain the Abyss that was the Sea?

Meredith was an elder. A water spirit. She'd seemed to think it was done.

Skye had her doubts. That was the role of air spirits. To think deeply and ask questions that no one wanted to hear.

And the missing air elementals, where had they gone? She'd felt the absence of other sylphs since just after Egan was chosen as Luminary.

She flew for what must have been hours. Searching for answers that never came.

Skye was only left with more questions.

Also by Linda Jordan:
Notes on the Moon People
Bibi's Bargain Boutique
Infected by Magic
The Bones of the Earth Series Book 1: Faerie Unraveled
The Bones of the Earth Series Book 2: Faerie Contact

Coming Soon:
The Bones of the Earth Series Book 3: Faerie Descent
The Bones of the Earth Series Book 4: Faerie Flight
The Bones of the Earth Series Book 5: Faerie Confluence

Come on over to Linda's website and join the fun!
LindaJordan.net

Don't miss a release!
Sign up for Linda's Serendipitous Newsletter while you're there.

Faerie Contact

The Bones of the Earth

Book 2

Linda Jordan

Published by Metamorphosis Press
www.MetamorphosisPress.com

Copyright © 2016 by Linda Jordan
All rights reserved

ISBN-13:978-0997797114/ISBN-10:0997797118

This is a work of fiction. Names, characters, places or incidents are either the product of the author's imagination or are used fictitiously. Any resemblance to actual events, or persons, either living or dead, is entirely coincidental.

The Bones of the Earth

Book 2:

Faerie Contact

BY
LINDA JORDAN

For Michael & Zoe

Chapter 1 ~ Clare

Clare switched the store lights on, wincing from the brightness. The exotic and unmistakable scent of Nag Champa incense filled her nose. Marcella must have been burning it last night.

As if most of the tourists could tell the difference between types of incense. Better to burn the cheap stuff for them.

That was not kind, Clare told herself.

She closed and locked the door behind her, juggling the bank bag and her keys. The bell hanging near the top chimed delicately.

Tea. She desperately needed caffeine. What flavor should she have today?

The store looked mostly tidy. Books on their shelves took up half the store. The rest was filled with: crystals, candles, incense and burners and display cases containing beautiful silver and gold jewelry, much of it decorated with semiprecious stones. Hand drums, painted and not, hung high on the sky blue walls. In one corner a rack held beautiful velvet, hooded capes in a rainbow of colors.

Near the check stand was a box containing lavender caramels for sale. For spur of the moment purchases.

The front display window was full of local interest books about Glastonbury Tor, the Chalice Well, and the White Spring. Designed to appeal to the tourists. Tourist season was drawing to an end, she'd need to change the window soon. Figure out what would appeal to the local villagers.

She needed to step up her game.

It was quiet in the shop. She needed to get the music on. Soon, things would be bustling. Mornings were always rushed for her. She should probably get here earlier.

Clare walked into the back, flicked the hallway lights on and tapped in the numbers to turn off the alarm system. Then she went behind the main glass display counter, set the bank bag down on the chair and checked the messages. Only one, a supplier hoping to deliver today. She'd call back later when she could face talking to someone.

On the counter sat a pile of notes from Marcella. She always left behind notes about things that had gone wrong, customer requests and problems, and ideas for the store, many of them quite good. Plus a lot of clutter: books that needed to be shelved, an open pack of tarot cards, wrappers from the lemon candy that she loved and three very expensive crystals.

Which should be in the case.

Clare sighed. Marcella always left a mess when she worked. No matter how many times she'd been asked to clean up after herself.

In the back room, Clare hung up her purse on a hook and draped her tan jumper over it. She took the kettle into the loo and filled it with fresh water and back to the stockroom to plug it in. She pulled out a clean teapot and spooned some Irish Breakfast tea into it.

Clare pulled her current favorite mug off the rack. The turquoise one with the lovely painting of a green woman on it.

It had been a birthday gift from him.

Even though James was gone and her feelings for him still held an edge of bitterness, she loved the beautiful mug enough to overcome the connection.

She put some soft flute music on the store's sound system and glanced at the clock. Time to open.

Glancing longingly at the kettle which was still heating, she turned to the mirror, straightened the silver and jasper pendant around her neck. Pulled her tan blouse down and her tan slacks up. Ran a hand over her shoulder length hair, smoothing it. At least she looked neat and tidy. Like a well-run shop's owner should.

Clare went out to the front and unlocked the door.

She hadn't gotten her morning things done, but the tourists from the first buses would be descending soon. Opening the cash register drawer, she sorted the bills and coins into their slots and closed it. Then slid the empty bag onto the shelf beneath the counter, tossed the candy wrappers in the trash and picked up the crystals, returning them to their cases. She patted them lovingly.

She noticed four other large crystals were missing from the case. Perhaps Marcella had sold them last night.

Clare shelved the books, poured the hot water into the teapot, then went back in front to tidy up while the tea steeped. She managed to get her first cup poured before the first customers came in.

She perched on the chair behind the counter, cupping her warm mug with both hands. Cold hands, despite the sun shining outside.

Fall was coming. The mornings had a bite to them. Leaves were beginning to turn and the gardens she passed by on her way to work had that wan, worn-out look they always had in late, late summer.

The three older women looked like typical tourists. Dressed in colorful trousers with matching blouses and jumpers. Two of them carried small purses that hung like a rucksack, only over one shoulder and the other had one of those silly fanny packs on. Probably practical, but funny looking.

The women passed by the books quickly, made appreciative sounds near the crystals and jewelry. Then they saw the fairy houses. They oohed and aahed over those.

Another group came in and began to make the circuit of the store.

Clare closed her eyes and inhaled the scent of the tea, sipped it and tasted the fullness of the fermented leaves and the richness of the cream. Lovely, just lovely.

"Excuse me," asked one of the women. "If I buy this, can it be shipped to the US?"

"Of course," said Clare. "You'll just need to fill out an address label and pay shipping."

She'd learned quickly that it was worth the effort to provide the service.

"Oh, then I definitely want it," she said, setting the fairy house on one end of the counter and going back to the display.

"Well, I'm going to get one too," said the second woman.

The third woman went back to the crystals.

Clare pulled out a pad of address labels. The bell on the door signaled another group of people coming in the door.

It was going to be a busy morning. She should have called the supplier back when she first got in.

Clare turned on the lights for the large back room and went to get some shipping boxes for the fairy houses. Just where the wide hallway opened up into the back room, she noticed a large puddle ending in a trail of water on the floor.

Where had that come from?

She looked up at the high ceiling, but didn't see anything leaking from above. It hadn't rained for a week or two.

She followed it to the door of the small empty room and opened the door.

The trail of water led to the center of the floor.

The spare room was square and white, nothing special. It didn't even have windows. The floor was dark wood, far from perfect, but serviceable. In each of the four corners sat one of the crystals missing from the case.

Clare picked up the amethyst, white quartz, citrine and blue topaz, making a hammock out of bottom of her blouse to carry the fist sized stones in.

Sitting in the center of the room was a large chunk of opal she didn't recognize. Most of it was a yellow-brown color with blue swirling through it. A watery stone, the same size as the crystals, but she felt a heaviness from it, a power the others didn't carry.

Where had it come from? Maybe it belonged to Marcella. Clare picked it up and held it, catching a fleeting sensation of desperation as she did so, then added it to the pile of stones in her blouse.

She returned the four crystals to their case out front, except for the opal which she quickly put down by the bank bag, covering it with several paper bags. She didn't like the way it felt.

Clare checked on the customers and went back to find boxes. She'd mop up the water later, when there was a break from customers.

An hour later, Jenny got there.

"Sorry, I'm late. Me Mum didn't come on time. And Tom's sick," she said, taking off her black jumper and hurrying into the back room to hang it up.

"Life happens," said Clare.

She tried to keep the judgmental tone out of her voice. It wouldn't help anything. She knew from long experience that whatever staff she hired had faults and none of them seemed to have lives as ordered as her own.

"I'm going into the office to make a few phone calls. It's been busy so far," she said.

"Brilliant," said Jenny. She busied herself with tidying up the remaining faerie houses and chatting with customers.

Jenny's short, dark hair was mussed up. She had a plump, matronly appearance and people warmed to her, confiding in her and asking her opinion. And Jenny willingly gave them her opinions in such a way that it was always polite and often funny.

Clare envied her ease with customers. She'd been in retail for decades and still had to work hard to be that friendly to strangers. She had so much to learn.

Clare went to the back, poured herself another cup of tea, put a splash of cream in it and walked into the small office.

The room was painted apple green. The furnishings consisted of a wood desk, file cabinet and two wood straight chairs as well as a cushioned desk chair. There was a painting across from the desk, an oil of a pastoral scene. It looked down a hillside at hedgerows, a valley and the sky. The painting relaxed Clare. An electric heater stood in the corner. The room looked tidy and cozy.

Except that her desk was piled high with things which needed attention.

She made a note to talk to Marcella about the crystals and water this evening.

There were orders to put in, bills to pay, catalogs to look through to order more stock. Why did people still print catalogs anymore? Why didn't they just post them online and save a tree?

She returned the supplier's phone call, but he wasn't there. She left a message telling him, yes, please deliver.

Then called another supplier and talked her into giving the store a credit for their recent shipment of books, half of which had arrived bent, rumpled and torn. They'd been badly packed.

Then Clare called Kristin, the woman who made the fairy houses, asking for more. Kristin had another six ready, so she said she'd bring them by today. Tomorrow was Friday and the weekends were often busy, especially just before school started. People taking last minute vacations because summer was ending.

At one, Jenny left for the day. She only worked part time.

Clare was sitting in the shop, flipping through catalogs and marking things to order when the door chimed again. The chime sounded different, lighter and more trilling, which made her look up.

In walked a woman with blonde wavy hair down to her waist. She had blue-gray eyes and pale skin. She looked ethereal.

"Hello," said the woman.

"Hello," Claire replied.

"I'm looking for space to rent. I'm a massage therapist and energy worker and I need a workspace."

"And you have insurance and are all set up to work?"

"Yes," said the woman. "I've spent the last ten years working in the U.S., in Seattle. But I'm from the west of Ireland, so I'm familiar with the requirements here."

"Ah, I thought I recognized the accent," said Clare. "You don't do acupuncture or any other medical things, right? You know they require more thorough licensing."

"No, just massage therapy and energy work."

"The shop down the street has a man who does what he calls Faerie Healing. He makes a good living at it."

The woman smiled and said, "I'll have to check him out. It's not my thing though."

"I'm Claire Grigson. I own the shop," she said, extending her hand.

"I'm Skye O'Hanlon," said the woman, shaking it.

"Do you have a clientele here?"

"Not yet, although I had a following in Seattle."

"What brings you here then? To Glastonbury?"

"I needed a change of scene. Seattle's a very big city. And I've always wanted to live here."

Another one. A pilgrim who wanted to soak up the vibes from the Tor. Or the Chalice Well. Or the Goddess or the Faeries. Or the ley lines. There were so many spiritual seekers who came to live here, but they always moved on, never stayed.

Well, that's why she had a business, wasn't it? A revolving customer base.

"Do you have a place to live?" asked Clare.

"Yes, I've taken a room in a boarding house in town. I don't need much space."

"Well, I'll show you the room. It's just off the stock room, so it's fairly quiet. My staff will be told when it's occupied they need to be quiet back here."

Clare led Skye through the stock room to the back. "We open at 10:30 and close at five. In the summer, sometimes we close earlier if it's really slow."

"That works for me. I really don't want to work evenings anymore. I did enough of that in Seattle."

"We all need to have a life," said Clare.

So where was hers?

Skye said, "I don't have a bank account yet. I really prefer to do everything with cash. If I have a customer who can't do that, can I have them pay you with their plastic and have you pay me cash?"

"I don't have a problem with that."

They discussed the rental fee and agreed on an amount. Skye handed over the first and last month's rent in cash.

"Is it possible for me to paint the room?" she asked.

"It needs it, doesn't it? I'll tell you what, I'll pay for the paint if you pick it out. I've never liked the white. It was an office before I bought the store. There are brushes, tarps for the floor and supplies over in the maintenance cupboard there. And a ladder in the corner," Clare said.

"Perfect," said Skye. "I'll be back this afternoon with the paint."

"You are on top of things."

"I want to get started and it'll take some time for paint fumes to go away."

Clare nodded.

Skye left.

Clare sat and began going through catalogs again. She needed to get all her holiday orders in soon.

Things were looking brighter. Clare had a tenant for the room she'd never let before. It had always been part of the plan, but she'd never gotten around to fixing it up or advertising. She'd only had the shop for six months and was still figuring things out.

This would help take some of the pressure off.

Shortly afterwards, Kristin came in, lugging a big box filled with Faerie houses. The middle-aged heavy-set woman didn't look like someone who would make Faerie houses. She had short cut dark hair, speckled with gray. Her baggy jeans and trainers were topped by a bright purple T-shirt.

People who made Faerie houses should look like the massage therapist who just left, not like moms.

Clare helped her unload the little houses and place them on the display table. Each one was unique. Most were made of wood, sticks and twigs formed into unusual shaped dwellings with artful decorations.

"I got two more finished, so there's eight," said Kristin.

"Oh, I love this one," said Clare.

The house had a tiny porch made from twigs with some sort of cone the size of her fingernail used as the top for each of the rails. The porch had a minuscule chair on it, with soft green moss for the cushion.

"That's a fun one," said Kristin. "I am having such a lovely time making these."

"The tourists adore them. Keep making them please," said Clare, handing Kristin cash for them.

"My pocketbook loves them too. Looks like we get to go out to eat tonight."

"Let's hear it for not cooking," said Clare.

She knew Kristin was divorced with three boys. Cooking must really be something at her house. Boys were always hungry.

"So how's business otherwise?"

"It's coming along. I've never had a store before, always worked for someone else. I'm not sure what to expect. Especially since tourist season is winding down."

"Then you should offer things for the locals," said Kristin.

"I've been thinking about that. What things do you think I should do?"

"Programs. Lectures. You know, workshops."

"I don't have that much knowledge," said Clare.

"No one expects you to. But there are so many gifted people in the area who don't have a venue. You could provide that. Hold celebrations for the high holy days."

"Here, in the store? There's no room."

"I've seen the size of that back room. You're not using half of it. Do some rearranging and make a space back there. It wouldn't have to hold many, maybe twenty people. Make it an exclusive event. Charge a small fee to get in, enough to cover your costs and to pay the people leading it. You might have fun."

"I don't know anyone to ask to lead it. I've only lived here six months."

"I know several. I could introduce you. Tell me what sort of focus you want. I'll have you all over for tea and you can see if it's a fit. Make plans. It would be ever so much fun."

How long had it been since she'd had fun?

"Let me think about it. Figure out what it would take to make it happen."

"I'm not going to let this go, you know," said Kristin. "Your shop is so much nicer than the others. I want to see it succeed. The places that keep going here cater to the locals as well as the tourists."

"Thanks. I will think about it."

"It means you'd have to step out of your shell. Take the lead."

She'd already known that and it both excited and terrified her.

Buying and running her own store was a huge leap of faith in herself. But what Kristin was talking about was even larger. It was taking her some time to screw up her courage.

"Well, I've got to run. Need to pick the boys up. Do some soul searching and really think about this."

"I will. Thank you," said Clare.

After Kristin left, Clare went into the stock room. It would be easy enough to find the space in the store. She could decorate the walls with gauzy fabric and lights. Make it look magical, just as she had the front. After all, the front had been nothing but ugly bare walls when she moved in. She'd made it look beautiful.

So what was she afraid of?

Stepping out into the world and being seen by others? Then she'd have more work to do. It always happened that way.

Being responsible for whether other people were safe or even had a good time? She'd done that her entire childhood. Kept her sisters fed, clothed and helped with homework, while her parents drank themselves into a stupor every night.

Just remembering it brought back the sweet rot smell of wine. It made her stomach roil with nausea. She took a deep breath and sipped water from her mug.

She didn't want to be responsible for other people. She'd had enough of that and clearly wasn't any good at it. Look how both her younger sisters had turned out. Pregnant young, married young and always complaining about their lives, their kids, their husbands and being eternally broke.

Clara didn't want that life.

But what life did she want?

She wanted a life filled with love and joy, the love of a man who was her equal, not more, not less. She wanted to make a success of running her store, have enough money to travel, to buy what she wanted when she wanted to buy it, to pay her bills and to put a little away for the future. She had modest ambitions.

Clare glanced at the clock. Time to close up. She locked the front door, turned off the overhead lights, leaving just the twinkle lights on. Then emptied the register drawer and took the bank bag, money, checks and credit slips back into the office.

After she'd finished her accounting, Clare washed out her mug and set it on the rack to dry. Just as she was getting her jumper and purse, there was a knock on the front door.

Who could that be?

She peered around the corner to see Skye.

Clare unlocked the door.

"Hi, I know I'm late. It took me longer to get the paint than I expected. Can I just drop these off and then I'll start painting in the morning?"

"That would be fine," said Clare.

She let Skye in with her two cans of paint. Skye put them in her room and closed the door.

Clare picked up the bank bag, turned off all the lights and set the alarm.

Skye said, "I'm going out to eat, want to join me?"

Clare almost said no, then decided she should go. She needed to make some friends. Get out more. Her life was far too solitary.

"Where did you have in mind?"

"I passed a chip shop on the way back here and I've been craving them like crazy."

Clare's mouth watered at the thought. When was the last time she'd let herself eat something as unhealthy as fried chips and fish?

"Wonderful," she said.

Chapter 2 ◈ Skye

Skye bit into the fish and felt the heat. The fat and the rich tartar sauce filled her mouth. It tasted glorious. Food in Faerie was extraordinary, but sometimes humans did amazing things with it too. Still, she couldn't go as far as using the vinegar.

She sat back in the hard chair and looked around.

The Spiffy Chippy was full of people on their way home from work. Every table was taken and there was a line out the door of people getting orders to go.

Clearly, this was the place in town to come for a quick meal.

It was in a new building, the colors were more conservative than they would have been in a chip shop in Seattle. A bold navy and white checked tile floor that made her eyes want to cross. She preferred more subtle patterns. Navy seats on metal chairs and a shade darker table, also made of smooth metal.

The smells were what had caught her attention as she'd walked past on her way to Clare's shop to drop off the paint. Deep fried fish and chips. The rich scents had filled the sidewalk outside as she'd passed by. Luring her in.

Across the table Clare ate her chips, delicately dipping them in ketchup pooled in the cardboard box her order came in.

Skye sipped the cup of hot black tea, feeling it warm her all the way down to her belly. How long since she'd eaten?

Probably not today. She'd been out pounding the pavement all day. Making sure her licensing and insurance were all in order and then looking for likely places to set up her practice. She hadn't eaten last night either.

She needed to remember to take care of this human body which covered her own Fae body. It was tiresome. Her natural physical body was so much easier to care for. Sylphs didn't need much. A little concentrated food. Some water. And a lot of fresh air. Wind was her element.

"So, how long have you had the store?" she asked Clare.

The woman seemed so unobtrusive. Probably in her mid-thirties, she had dishwater blonde hair that stopped at the top of her shoulders, brown eyes and she was dressed all in tan clothes that washed out any color in her pale skin. She was nearly invisible. And her posture said she liked it that way, slightly hunched over, only occasionally making eye contact.

Skye longed to have a session with her, make her open up and watch her blossom.

"I just opened it six months ago."

"Really? It looks like it's been there for ages."

"That's the look I was going for. I wanted to look established, but I also wanted to appeal to novelty. Have new displays float through a couple times a month."

"It's a lovely store."

"A few of the locals think I should hold events there, but I'm a bit torn about that."

"What sort of events?"

"Speakers, rituals."

"Why are you torn? It seems like a natural thing."

"It means putting myself out there in a way I've never done before."

"Change is always challenging for us humans. Even though it's a normal part of life," Skye said, lying about the "us humans" part.

"I know. I'm just afraid."

"Of what?" asked Skye.

She sipped her tea, loving the heat, feeling it to the core of the human body. Her Fae body rarely felt cold, she was a sylph after all.

"Of looking stupid, of failing, of alienating customers."

"Well, that sounds pretty normal. I will tell you one thing though, in my not so vast experience, when we're called to do something that looks like a big challenge to us, but it seems the right thing to do, then not doing it is like taking a step backwards. And if you keep going backwards, then that's just dying a slow death."

"I know what you mean. I've done that too often in my life. I really don't want to do it anymore."

Skye chewed on one of the chips, dipped in ketchup. She'd grown accustomed to using ketchup in Seattle.

"Then it looks like you've already made a decision."

"I guess I have. I'm just afraid to move forward with it."

"You seem like a person who needs to plan and organize things before you move forward."

"Yeah."

"So, plan out a schedule. Figure out what you'd be comfortable with. Then adapt as needed."

Skye sent a small surge of energy in Clare's direction. A shot of courage and clarity. not large enough for Clare to realize it came from outside of herself, but enough to make a difference.

"You make it sound so simple when you put it like that."

Skye laughed. "That's because I'm on the outside, looking in. My life is rarely that simple. It looks all muddled."

Her life was definitely not simple. A sylph masquerading as a human. An air spirit trying to ease the way for the rest of Faerie. To prepare humans for the shock that they weren't alone on this lovely green and blue planet. That they never had been. They had just lived in denial of other beings' presence for several hundred years.

And now that Faerie's boundaries had been opened that transition needed to happen quickly. It couldn't take decades. And Faerie didn't want war. But humans were dangerous once cornered. They were a paranoid lot and easily threatened. At least that's what their history said. Skye liked to think that as individuals they were decent. But as a group, they were pretty scary.

She, and the others who'd volunteered for the same task, had much work ahead of them.

Clare pushed her cardboard plate away from her.

"I'm stuffed. I can't remember when I last ate so much, and such unhealthy food. But it tasted wonderful."

"I know. You've got to do it now and again. Can't live on a diet of veggies and bland food," said Skye.

"No, you can't and I've tried for far too long. So let's do this again. Or maybe curry next time?"

"I love curry. Just let me know when it works for you. I have kitchen privileges where I'm living, but I'm not fond of cooking."

"Deal," said Clare.

After they finished and left the chippy, the two of them walked through the crisp evening towards their homes. They both went the same direction for quite a ways.

The fog had come in, apparently that was common here. With it came a misting shower that felt cool. It soaked through Skye's hoodie and jeans in little time. She said good night to Clare at a corner, then turned and walked four more long blocks to the three story brick boarding house.

The front door was still unlocked and she entered, closed it and went up the narrow stairs to the attic, passing by the crowded common room.

She unlocked the door to her room and went in, closing it behind her and locking it. She could smell the dried lavender she'd brought from Faerie, sitting in a paper cup near her bed. She sighed, releasing the stress of being around so many humans all day.

Privacy. Something she'd come to value while living among humans. It was so necessary for her survival. A place where she could hide and be herself. This small, cozy room at the top of the house was a sanctuary for her in the human world.

She switched on the small bedside lamp, stripped off her wet clothes and hung them over the metal bed frame at the foot of her bed.

Then she pulled on a pair of soft cotton PJs with dragonflies printed on them and sat crosslegged in the big comfy chair in the corner, the peaked ceiling of the room slanting just over her head. The room felt warm and delicious, but it took some time to get her human body warm again.

She'd need to get some thicker waterproof clothes. She'd need this human body for some time.

Skye longed to leave her human body in the chair and go flying. But she worried about it, the temperature was still too cold. Human bodies were so fragile.

She missed the freedom of flying, of being light enough to float on the breeze. Skye missed the company of her own kind, but she was used to that. She'd only had other Fae nearby for the last several months. Before then she hadn't seen another Fae for nearly a thousand years. Ever since she'd left Faerie the first time.

But even when she'd returned a few months ago and the boundaries of Faerie were unraveled, the other air spirits had vanished. Fleeing from Egan's fire. He was the new

Luminary and it had taken him quite a while to get his heat under control.

The strange thing was that the other air spirits hadn't returned. Had they been devoured by the Formorians' winds? It wasn't the first time she'd considered the possibility. She sensed an emptiness that couldn't be accounted for.

The breezes and winds whispered nothing to her. As if they were lifeless. Never in her long life had she felt such a vacuum.

And it alarmed her.

Did the other elementals feel the same thing?

She was the first to venture out into the world after the fall of the boundaries and the imprisonment of the Formorians, the old primordial gods.

Had they taken large parts of Faerie with them, as they'd planned?

She had no answers and a million questions.

Perhaps once she'd settled in and was earning money again, a trip back to Faerie would be possible. Just to check in and see if anyone else felt the same emptiness.

Chapter 3 ∞ Clare

Clare unlocked the door. She smelled Nag Champa again.

Was someone breaking in? How could they get past the alarm system? Was it even working? Perhaps she should call the company and have them do a test.

Maybe she needed to invest in better locks, even though she'd purchased a brand new deadbolt before opening the shop. And only two other people had keys. Which reminded her, she needed to get a key for Skye.

She'd forgotten to call Marcella last night and ask about the water and the crystals. She'd been too tired.

Clare put the kettle on and the money in the cash register drawer. Then she walked around the store, looking for things that might be out of place. She moved some books around and noticed crystals missing from the case again.

She went in the back towards Skye's room. There were pools of water on the floor again. She opened the door. The crystals and opal were back where they'd been yesterday morning, forming four corners. Another pool of water in the center.

Clearly, someone or something had been there. She shivered.

"That's just silly," she said, pushing the idea of a ghost or some other spirit out of her head.

There had to be a simple explanation. She picked up the stones and put them back in the case and the opal on the shelf beneath the cash register. She still got a feeling of desperation from the stone. She wasn't that sensitive to rocks, not like some people, but this one spoke to her. And she didn't like the message. She covered it with the empty bank bag.

Then listened to the messages. There was one from Kristin. She was trying to set up a tea with Clare, and two of her friends. Would next Sunday work?

Had Kristin known Clare usually took that day off and let Jenny work?

She'd get back to her later.

It was time to open the store.

Today, Marcella was on time, a rare occurrence. She was ready to work when the tourists arrived. Clare mopped up the water again. She'd need to call someone to take a look at the roof. The water had to be coming from there, even though she didn't see any leaks. The pooled water was too far away from any of the plumbing. She should talk to Marcella first.

Skye came in not long afterwards. As she entered the tourists stared at her. The woman really was quite extraordinary to look at. She looked as if she'd stepped out of a Renaissance painting and slipped into jeans and a T-shirt. Her features were perfect and the long blonde wavy hair was thick and eye-catching.

Skye seemed oblivious. She waved at Clare and headed towards the back room, while Clare rung up some jewelry for a customer.

When Clare was finished, she went into the back. Skye had found the paint tarps and laid them across the floor. She had the ladder set up and was carrying a brush from the storage cabinet.

"Good morning," she said.

"Good morning," said Clare. "Are you finding everything?"

"I am." Skye set the brush down on the ladder and began braiding her hair into one long braid, then wrapped the end with a hair tie she took off her wrist.

"You have such lovely hair."

"Thank you. I've never had short hair like yours, it must be much easier to deal with."

"Except that I wake up every morning with bed head and have to soak it to get it to do anything."

Skye laughed.

"What colors did you get?" asked Clare.

"I got this lovely salmon/peach color and a pale yellow ochre. I'll sponge that on to give some texture. And put it on the ceiling."

"That'll be beautiful."

"I wanted something warm and comforting. People need the feeling of warmth when they've got nothing on but a sheet. I'll bring a heater and a heated massage table pad, but anything I can do to help them loosen up their muscles helps."

"And I wanted to do the opposite out in front. Give the tourists a cool, calm place to come to."

"I love the blues and aquas you used out there. It almost feels like being underwater. It's what first drew me into the store," said Skye. "I think it's perfect."

"Thanks. Well, I'd better get back out front. There's a fan over there, if you want it. I'll open the front door once it warms up a bit. Let some of the paint smell out. When you get up to the ceiling, could you feel if its wet?"

"No problem. If it is, it wouldn't take the paint anyway, right?"

"You're probably right."

Clare went back out front just as the next bunch of customers came in.

The morning was busy. She only managed to get out of the front of the store for an hour to work on orders and the accounts. Then after Clare ate a quick lunch of roast chicken and salad greens in the office, Marcella left.

Clare remembered, after Marcella left, that she hadn't gotten a chance to ask about the water and crystals. Her excitement about creating events had made her unable to concentrate.

The afternoon was quieter. Clare sat down with a pad of paper and roughed out a schedule for possible events. The first would be on October 31, All Hallow's Eve or Samhain.

About a month and a half from now.

She'd have to put in some extra hours to move the back room around. To create a space. There was a lot of shelving back there with extra stock on it. She needed to compress that area. And put screens up or something to hide the mess.

The phone rang and she answered.

"The Sacred Space, this is Clare."

"Oh, hello Clare. This is Kristin. I was wondering if you got my message."

"Kristin, sorry I didn't call you back. It's been crazy busy today."

"I understand. The sun's out, everyone's spending money. Will Sunday work for you?"

"Yes, it will. I'd be happy to come. And thank you for arranging it. Oh, and while I've got you on the phone, I need more fairy houses when you've got some."

"I've got a couple more. I'm going to really get ahead of things this winter. Make a lot of them. I just can't seem to keep up with the demand."

"That would be a great idea. It's not as if we get a lot of repeat business from the tourists. So your houses will always be new to them. I don't see this trend dying down any time soon."

"Good. Because I've got to keep these kids in shoes and they're growing like weeds. See you on Sunday. Oh and feel free to bring any of your staff if they'd like to come."

"Great. I'll come with my ideas."

Clare went back to planning out the bones of the calendar. She'd have celebrations on the four high holidays: Samhain, Imbolc, Beltane and Lammas. Then on the solstices and equinoxes.

Next she needed to make a list of locals or sort of local writers who lived near and see if she could get any of them to come out and give workshops. There were several people who'd created tarot decks or who she'd heard gave workshops of their own. Perhaps they'd like to use her space.

And finally, she needed to start a mailing list of local people who might want to come for events. She'd put off doing that for far too long. Just like she'd put off the rest of her life.

Time for that to stop.

Skye appeared from the back room. The woman hadn't even taken a lunch break.

"I think I'm done. Want to come look?"

Clare slid her papers under the counter and followed Skye into the back. The paint fumes were really noticeable. She needed another fan to push the smelly air out the front door.

Skye's room looked quite lovely. She'd already done the base coat as well as the sponging and ceiling. She'd even put the ladder and tarps away.

"Beautiful," said Clare.

"I think it turned out quite nicely," said Skye.

Skye didn't have one drop of paint on her either.

Clare could never do that. She always managed to get more paint on herself than on what she was painting.

"I'll let it air out for a day and then bring my table and supplies in. Can you let the staff know that I'll do free massages for them for the next week, when they're not working? And for you too, of course."

"I will. That's very generous."

"The way I work is different from most practitioners. I've found it helps to experience what I do in order to communicate it to people who might interested. Tomorrow I'll work on getting a flyer and cards printed up with my website address. That's where I take reservations."

"Great, I'll find a place up front where we can put them. Say, I'm going over to have tea at Kristin's on Sunday. She makes the fairy houses that we sell. Anyway, she's got a couple of friends who have ideas about events at the store. I wondered if you might like to come along. Add in your ideas."

"Oh, that would be lovely. Thank you," said Skye.

"I'll let her know. I can meet you here, she just lives a few blocks away."

"Perfect. Then I can bring a load of stuff here."

"Do you have a car?"

"I don't drive."

"Would you like me to help you move in?"

"Really, it's no trouble. I'm happy making several trips. It's part of my workout regime. I'll be buying a new heater, some furniture and the music player new anyway. I've been looking just down the street and found a lot of it."

"Well, let me know if you need help."

"I'll do that," said Skye.

The phone rang. Claire ran to answer it out in front, instead of in the office. It was Jenny.

"Hi, I just wanted to see if you needed me tomorrow. I have to take Alex to his match at ten. I could come in after that. Another parent will bring him home."

"That would be fine. Marcella's coming in tomorrow morning too."

"I'll see you then," said Jenny.

"Wait, I'm just wondering if you've been burning any Nag Champa."

"Me no, I hate incense. Never burn it. I use the aromatherapy oils instead."

"And you haven't moved crystals into the small room in back and left them there?"

"Not me."

"And this hunk of opal isn't yours?"

"No. I'll take a look at it when I come in tomorrow, but I never bring my stones into the store. Why?"

"Things have been out of place when I came in the last two mornings. And the smell of Nag Champa's in the air. There are pools of water on the floor in the back. It's not me. It's not you. It could be Marcella, but…"

"Wow. Maybe someone from the last business still has a key."

"I put a new lock on when I took over. And the alarm system's new. I just don't understand."

"Wow. That's creepy. Have they done any damage or nicked anything?"

"Not that I've seen. I need to look around some more. I think we should all be paying attention to when we see things out of place."

"I'll do that. See you tomorrow then?"

"Yes."

Clare hung up.

Skye was on her way out the door.

"I'll see you tomorrow," said Skye. "I'll start bringing stuff in."

"Okay," said Clare.

She spent the rest of the day poking around near the front windows and door, looking for openings. Examining the walls in the back room. There were no openings in the ceilings or floors.

In the end, she found nothing.

But she was left with a feeling of violation. Someone was intruding on her space. It was all the more worrying that she had no idea who it was and what they wanted. It left a nagging tension that centered right between her shoulders and weighed on her like a massive metal anchor.

Chapter 4 ~ Skye

Skye left the Claire's store and headed down the street past all the brightly colored shopfronts. The narrow sidewalks were crowded. Another bus must have pulled in.

The town's population seemed to ebb and flow. The place must be completely mad in June when the rock festival happened.

The breeze picked up and the wind bit through her light jacket. She turned and continued towards the Chalice Gardens. The day was dwindling into late afternoon.

Skye stretched out as she walked, taking longer strides and rolling her shoulders, sore from all the painting. Her Fae body would never get sore muscles from a day of painting.

She would be able to start her work on Monday, which thrilled her. Even though her real work had already begun.

Infiltrating the human community. At least the parts of it who might already believe that Faerie existed.

Tomorrow would be interesting.

Skye paid her admission and walked into the gardens. She closed her eyes and breathed in the sweet scent of some flower. The area was filled with lots of different flowers but she had no idea which ones the smell came from and probably couldn't have named it anyway.

This place was filled with magic, human magic. The kind that came from faith and belief. It wasn't as powerful or showy as Fae magic, but it belonged here. The water that flowed into the Chalice well was sacred in a way that only humans could make it.

She continued down the path made of gray stones, passing several people who were leaving.

The bulk of tourists were probably gone for the day as it neared dinnertime.

Her stomach growled. She'd forgotten lunch.

Skye sighed.

It was so difficult for her to stay in touch with this human body. No wonder so many of her human clients weren't really in their bodies. Human bodies were always in some sort of discomfort so people lived in their minds. Human bodies were always hungry, hurting or tired. Rarely did they feel nice.

Her normal self, her Fae body was generally in a state of ecstasy. Thrilled with the slightest breeze brought in from the sea, the sight of a raven flying, the scent of apple blossoms, the feeling of her wings flying through the chill air. Her sylph body rarely hurt, hardly ever felt hunger and almost never felt tired.

How did humans survive? How could they laugh when they were so weighed down with heaviness of their lives?

When Skye saw the massive yews, there was a slight thickness near one of the trunks. She could see the energetic presence of a Fae, standing out against the shimmer of the well-loved trees. The trees radiated a sort of health and vitality.

Adaire moved away from them, probably sensing Skye's presence.

The body she wore was the same as the last human one Skye had seen her in. She guessed Adaire always made the same body. She was a creature of habit. The body was medium height, slender, but muscular. Dark hair and eyes. It looked as earthy as Adaire's real self was.

Adaire was a dryad, an earth spirit. Most at home in the forest, being one with the trees.

Skye moved towards her, arms out.

Adaire hugged her firmly.

"It's so good to see you. I've missed your smile."

"It's lovely to see you too," said Adaire. "Can you believe how big these yews have gotten? I haven't visited them in a very long time."

Skye nodded.

"So, how are things going for you?" asked Adaire.

"Good, I've found a place to live, the attic of a boarding house. And I'm creating a massage space in a New Age shop. The Sacred Space. I think things will work out splendidly."

"Good, because my work will reach a lot fewer people. I'm working with a forestry crew. They love the trees, but believing in Fae will be a tough sell."

"How long since you left Faerie?" asked Skye.

"Three days ago. This time. I started looking for work before you left. It takes some time to get hired on."

"How was everything in Faerie?"

Adaire shrugged. "Good. Egan's doing all the right things. Some of the water spirits were still struggling with the idea of having a fire spirit running things. But he's not pushing them."

Skye said, "Things are strange here. Maybe it's just this part of the world, maybe I just grew used to being in Seattle. Maybe it's this particular body I'm in. But things feel off."

"Off?"

"Energy wise. Every human body I make is tapped into the energy fields. I need to for my work. This body is the most sensitive one I've made so far. It's really close to my natural self. Anyway I can feel something rumbling below the normal energy levels. It feels deep, strong and powerful. I can't see more than that. I don't understand what it is and I've never felt anything like this. Ever."

"The Formorians felt like that to me."

"Possibly. I wasn't in a human body when I felt them." The alarm she felt drained her energy. Skye sensed that she always needed to be on guard. It was more than just masquerading as human. Everything felt heavy and hard these days.

"Well, someone will be passing by soon to get information from us and take it back to Egan. Tell them what you're feeling. Perhaps Meredith will have some ideas. Or one of the other elders. They're beginning to return you know."

"Are they?"

The news lightened Skye's heart a bit. The elders had begun to wither away in the long centuries Faerie was closed to the rest of the world.

"Yes, but not all of them. Some of them were just too far gone, I think. Those just continue to fade."

"I still don't know where all the air spirits have gone to."

"I'm sorry. It must make you feel very alone."

"It does. I returned to Faerie hoping for the company of my own kind. And they all fled and have vanished."

Grief flowed through her again and she closed her eyes, breathed in the fragrant humousy air and breathed out. Allowing the pain to flow out of her.

It didn't do any good to carry it around. Skye had learned that from all the humans she worked on. They held onto so much pain and sadness. It kept them stuck. She couldn't afford to do that and continue to do her work.

The energy demanded to flow and she needed to do her work, quickly. Egan wasn't promising her years to make contact here. Anything could happen and she had a foreboding that it would. That her time here in Glastonbury would be cut short. Both she and Adaire needed to make quick work with tasks that required months of delicacy.

Her stomach rumbled loudly.

She really did need to pay attention to her body.

"I'd better move along. This body needs to eat."

"I'm going to stay. These trees are so beloved by everyone. It's nice to hang out with them. They have so much to say," said Adaire.

"All right. I'll touch base with you next week?"

"Sounds wonderful. I've missed you," said Adaire.

"I missed you as well," said Skye hugging her.

Then Skye made her way back to the entrance and out.

She passed through the busy section of town again, trying to figure out what her body wanted and settled on a burger and tea.

She sat at a small table in the corner of the small shop, decorated in a garish combination of red, blue and yellow. The seats and tables were plastic. Everything screamed: "buy lots, eat fast and get out so someone else can take your place." Sometimes the human world was magical, other times it was simply jarring.

Unwrapping her burger from the paper wrapper, she took a huge bite, tasting the greasy meat, ketchup, mustard and pickle. The flavors mingled gloriously. Skye couldn't remember the last time she'd eaten a burger.

The noise of people chattering away at their tea time after a busy day filled the room. A busy week. She'd nearly forgotten it was Friday night. The vast majority of people around her were off work for the weekend.

But not the fast food workers or the shopkeepers. Or her.

Tomorrow, she'd start moving into her new space. How fun!

She was looking forward to decorating. But she really should wait till Monday to hang things on the wall. Let the paint have a good dry.

Skye had bought a lovely small table with two drawers, at one of the antique dealers. It would be perfect to hold her small music system and an incense burner. She'd ended up buying a dresser, a gorgeous lamp and a wooden chair from the same dealer. And gotten some old brass hooks mounted on a wooden strip so clients could hang up their clothes.

She'd bring in her massage table, the warming pad and a covered woven basket to collect used sheets until she took them to the launderette. And she still needed to buy that sound system and the small heater.

Then, she'd shop the new age shops for artwork to decorate with. Clare had some wonderful prints. She'd start there.

Skye finished her burger, cleaned up the wrappings and tossed them in the trash as she walked out the door. She sipped her hot tea while walking home.

The breeze had a chill to it. The leaves were turning deeper colors every day and beginning to drop off the trees. Swirling and gathering into little columns of whirlwinds.

She smiled. This really was the best time of year.

If only she could figure out why everything felt so wrong.

Chapter 5 ~ Clare

Sunday morning Clare slept in. Marcella was opening and closing the store today. Jenny was coming in later to help her. Having a day off felt wonderful.

If only she hadn't agreed to go to Kristin's for tea.

Clare sat up, swinging her feet down onto the wood floor. The coldness shocked her. She really should get a bedside rug one of these days.

She felt around for her slippers and slid into them. Giving a deep sigh, she stood and pulled the bedding up. Straightening the tan cotton bedspread and tucking everything in.

In the kitchen, she filled the kettle with fresh water and plugged it in. She spooned some black tea with lavender and bergamot into a teapot. Waited for the water to boil. Rubbing her hands over her face, trying to wake up.

She switched on the mobile dock and played some fiddle music, Alastair Frazier. His fiddle soared around the piano accompaniment, swooped beneath it and then up again, strong and flexible.

The small kitchen was tidy from last night. Clare liked her house clean and organized. Just like the shop. She'd had roommates for so many years, while trying to save money, and those shared living quarters never suited her.

Now that she owned her own home, she could keep things exactly the way she liked them. The cleanliness gave her a sense of peace that she'd longed for her entire life. Within her sparsely furnished home, she brought home a few choice objects merely to add beauty.

The tiled counters weren't covered with crumbs from someone else's meal. The floor had been hoovered recently. The table wasn't covered with a week's worth of mail. But instead had a vase containing prickly branches with scarlet leaves and interesting seed stalks she'd gleaned from hedgerows on a recent walk. Her window looked out into a tiny back garden, that was empty, and a wooden fence for privacy. A modest home, but one within her means.

Clare poured the hot water over the tea and smelled the lavender and tea leaves. She put the lid on the tea pot. Then poured some rolled oats into a bowl, covered it with milk. She pulled a few sections of cut up plums out of a freezer container and put them on the oats. Then stuck it in the microwave and waited, checking her mobile for messages and email. No messages from the shop, always a good sign.

She poured and sipped the hot tea and ate porridge with plums and milk for breakfast. Then vacuumed and cleaned her already clean, small house. Like she did every week.

After showering, she dressed in a pair of loose jeans, a purple T-shirt and short leather boots.

By 12:30 she was heading out toward the shop to meet Skye. At least she'd have company and a supporter.

Why did she have the feeling that she was about to be pushed and shoved around? That Kristin and her friends had an agenda already planned out?

One that she wouldn't agree with.

The spiritual communities in this area, maybe everywhere, were a minefield. It was so easy to step on someone's toes.

She'd worked hard to avoid that.

She got to the shop a bit early. It was quite crowded for a Sunday lunchtime. She waved at Jenny and Marcella who were busy with customers.

Then went into the office and listened to messages. There weren't any. Which pleased her.

She opened the desk drawer, took out her small notebook with the event ideas in it and slipped it plus a pen into her shoulder bag.

Skye walked past and said, "I'm here. Just gotta drop these off."

Clare followed her, noticing she carried a stack of neatly folded sheets. Skye's leather boots clunked on the hardwood floor. Over her jeans, she wore a long brown coat that looked like one of the dusters cowboys wore in the movies.

The paint smell had dissipated and was replaced with the scent of a subtle earthy incense. Not Nag Champa. And the floor was dry. But perhaps Jenny or Marcella mopped up. She'd have to ask them.

She hadn't seen the room since Skye had finished painting. It was completely transformed.

"Wow, this is wonderful. Will you come decorate my house?" Clare said.

There was an old dark wooden dresser with drawers that Skye put the sheets in. It was topped with an antique table lamp, the stained glass shade made of pieces of green and yellow ochre glass. And a small music player.

Another wooden table held Skye's business cards on a slightly tarnished silver plate. With plenty of room for a client's purse and mobile. Nearby sat an old wooden chair. There were hooks on the wall next to the chair. A large portable heater sat in one corner.

The massage table sat in the center of the small room.

Each of the four walls had a piece of art on it. The east wall had a hanging of birds' feathers, woven yarns and iridescent glass. The south wall, a ceramic mosaic glass piece of a blazing sunset. On the west wall hung a sculpture of driftwood, shells and beach glass. The last wall contained a weaving made from what looked like moss, reeds and rushes of a forest scene.

"These are gorgeous."

"I was going to go with prints, until I found these at one of the antique shops. They're made by a local artist."

"Everything works so well together."

"The four elements always have. When there's balance," said Skye. "I was going to wait to put them up tomorrow. To give the paint extra time to dry. But it was perfectly dry yesterday and I couldn't wait to see what it all looked like."

"Did you carry all this furniture?"

"No, they delivered it. Except for the massage table. It folds up. I carried that. Like I said, workout regime. I've got to get back into shape. Massage is hard physical work."

"It's stunning. And it feels cozy and warm. I think your clients will love it."

"I hope so," said Skye, smiling.

"Well, are you ready to go?"

"Yep."

They left the room and Skye closed the door, locking it behind her.

Clare sighed as they walked back towards the front of the store. She wasn't looking forward to this tea. No, it was worse than that. She was dreading it.

Clare waved at Jenny and Marcella as they left the store.

"I'm looking forward to meeting Kristin. I like her little houses," said Skye.

"She's quite a character," said Clare.

They walked a little farther down the main street before turning off. The fog hadn't lifted yet and it had a chilly dampness to it that made Clare zip her coat a bit higher, tightening the neck beneath her short hair.

"I have to tell you," said Clare, "I'm a little uncomfortable with this meeting. I have a sense that Kristin and her friends are going to be a bit pushy."

"Let them push. You're strong enough to stand up for what you believe in. It's your store after all. Your identity on the line."

"Thanks. I really don't like to make a fuss."

"Sometimes it's necessary. Otherwise people who are oblivious don't realize they've reached the edge of your boundaries."

Clare laughed.

"I've known a lot of oblivious people in my life."

"Haven't we all?" said Skye, laughing.

She reminded Clare of a piercing beam of sunlight, unfolding everything with stark clarity.

Kristen lived in a brick rowhouse, the most common type of house Clare had seen in Glastonbury. She was still a relative newcomer.

Before Clare even got a chance to knock on the door, Kristin opened it. She was wearing a bulky navy jumper, jeans and wool clogs.

"Welcome," she said.

"Good afternoon," said Clare. "Kristin, this is Skye. She's a massage therapist who's set up her space in the store."

"Hello Skye."

"Hi Kristin."

"Well, come in, please." said Kristin, showing them in through the hallway to a dining room.

"I thought we could meet in here where there's a big table."

"Great," said Clare.

The house smelled wonderful. The scent of something baked with butter filled the air.

There were three women sitting at the table already. Peeking out from beneath a white tablecloth embroidered with flowers in red, oranges and yellows, the wood table was so dark it was nearly black. Six matching chairs sat around it. The table and chairs looked incredibly elegant.

Kristin had set the table with stoneware painted with bright yellow and orange nasturtiums. Red napkins were topped with silverware and the glassware was clear with yellow rims. The table was completed by a magnificent bouquet of bright red dahlias, twisted bare branches and yellow-leaved grass with abundant dried tassels. Everything looked very cheery.

The dining room was painted a yellow ochre color and the art that hung on the walls was clearly made by someone's children. Drawings made on wrinkled paper, finger paintings in bright colors framed with department store frames.

The furniture may have been formal, but the tone of the room said it was a well lived-in space and it felt casual. Was the table inherited?

"Well," said Kristin. "I'll introduce everyone. This is Clare, who owns the Sacred Space. And Skye who does massage there. This is Miranda, she's a painter." Kristin gestured to a thin, muscular-looking woman wearing a red T-shirt, jeans and black cowboy boots with fancy skulls on them.

"And Emma, she owns The Goddesses' Garb, along with sewing most of the clothing sold there." Emma wore a silky purple tunic over black leggings and black suede boots. The tunic had a spiral design sprinkled with white flowers on it.

Had Emma made that one? It was lovely. Clare would have liked to sell it at her own shop.

Emma waved at them.

Kristin continued, "And Raven, she's a tarot reader and writer."

Raven had wild, mostly dark hair, interspersed with streaks of silver that made her pearly skin look even paler. She looked delicate and her loose black turtleneck and bulky silver and stone jewelry did little to dispel the effect.

Everyone said hello, while Kristin poured tea. Sandwiches and clear glass plates of green salad were passed around.

Kristin said, "I hope the food works for everyone. I didn't know if anyone had restrictions. The sandwiches are tuna, egg salad, and roasted red pepper with cucumbers. No dairy and no meat. But there's definitely butter in the shortbread cookies." She pointed to a plate of pale cookies cut out in the shape of moons.

"Thank you, this is lovely," said Skye.

"Wonderful," said Claire.

They ate, making small talk about the cooling weather and the dwindling glorious summer.

Emma asked, "When did you open your practice Skye?"

Skye said, "I haven't yet. I plan to work a little next week. A soft opening. Doing massages for the staff. Get my mojo going again. You're all welcome to come in for free, just make a reservation on my website for next week. The following week, after the twentieth, you'll have to pay though. That's when I begin in earnest."

She put a stack of her business cards on the table and everyone took one.

"Oh, I love a massage," said Emma. "My back gets so sore, hunched over the sewing machine all the time."

"I can help with that," said Skye, smiling and picking up her cup of tea to sip.

Clare was thinking Skye might bring a few extra customers into the shop. She was so magnetic, people were drawn to her immediately. She had a sense of otherworldliness about her. Marcella had called her fey.

When the lunch plates were taken away, cookies passed around and more tea poured, Kristin said, "I think we should get started."

Everyone nodded. Then Miranda spoke.

"Well, I've lived in this area for twenty years and seen lots of businesses come and go. The ones that are long lived provide a service for the locals. Because the bulk of the tourist season is only about six months out of the year. I love your store Clare, but I think the thing that you're missing is events for the people who live here. The other metaphysical stores in town all provide that. Although their rituals or gatherings are slanted to their own particular audience. One serves the old-school esoterics, another the Buddhists and another the really woo woo New Agers."

"No one serves us," said Emma.

"Who's us?" asked Skye.

"The Goddess followers," said Raven.

"I'm new here. What about the old-school esoterics? Don't they follow the Goddess?" asked Skye.

"Not the same thing," said Emma. "They're very patriarchal based. All of their rituals have that at their foundations."

Raven nodded, "It's really quite twisted when you look into it deeply, it's as if they want to own or control the Goddess."

"That's why we call them old-school. They came into being a century or two ago. Some were trying to recapture the ancient Pagan traditions, others the Druidic ones. But their roots were formed in such patriarchal eras. It's built into the structure of everything they do," said Miranda.

Clare just sat and listened, sipping her tea and nibbling on the buttery shortbread.

"We need a regular place to hold our rituals. Inside. Because we're all feeling a little old to be out cavorting in the rain on Yule," snorted Kristin.

"There's more than just us. But we don't have a central location, a permanent gathering place, so we can only gather three or four at a time. And have no place to point newcomers to," said Raven.

"What do you think?" asked Emma.

Clare set down her teacup and said, "I've worked at a lot of businesses in my life. And I've watched divisiveness destroy many of them. This is the first business that I've actually owned. And I've worked hard to make sure it's inclusive of everyone and every spiritual path. I don't want to undo all that work."

Clare didn't say it, but she didn't want to offend the Christian mystics who came to her shop. Even though they did have other places to shop. They apparently liked her book selection.

Miranda said, "I can understand that. So reach out to other groups and invite them in as well. There are others not being served. The 'Airy Fairy' people have no place to go either. And there's a couple major fairy artists in town. You're already selling Kristin's fairy houses."

Clare said, "The problem is that I'm so new here, I don't know anyone."

Raven said, "I do."

Kristin laughed and said, "Raven knows everyone. Either through reading tarot cards, or her boys' football teams, or her garden club, or her volunteer work."

Raven said, "It's true."

"Do you know any local writers or other people who'd like to present a program?" asked Clare.

"I do," said Raven. "Let me make a list."

She began writing on a pad of paper in front of her.

"I have a couple names for you too," said Miranda.

"You know," said Emma, "the whole inclusive thing might work. It does for the Chalice Well Trust and their Wheel of the Year celebrations, but I really think you can't please everybody. They don't go deep enough"

Skye said, "At least not all at the same time."

Emma nodded. "Everyone wants to go deeper in their own traditions."

Clare still wasn't convinced this was the right thing to do.

They talked more about what the group wanted in terms of space and time.

Clare said, "I'll need to think about all this. And rough out a schedule. I'll let you know in a week. I'm sure it takes time to put together a ritual and get the word out."

Emma said, "You know, I think it's important that we rent the space from you. Either you'll have to be there or you'll have to pay one of your staff to open and close the store. Why don't you think about what it costs you to keep the store open? Any sales would just be gravy."

Clare nodded. She'd vaguely realized there would have to be someone staffing any events she had the store open for. And if she wanted to participate in the event, then it might not work for that person to be her.

Afterwards, she and Skye walked down the sunny sidewalks. It was almost warm outside with the fog gone.

"Well, that went better than I expected," said Clare.

"No one can push you around unless you let them," said Skye.

"Miranda and I don't get along all that well. When I first opened, she tried to push me into buying her paintings to sell. I love her work, but they're too expensive for my shop. I'm not an art gallery. She and I haven't gotten along since."

Skye didn't say anything.

"It was very generous of you to offer free massages to them next week."

"Gotta get the word out. I put a notice out on my mailing list, so Seattle people who are traveling can find me here. But basically, I'm beginning all over again."

"That's got to be tough."

"I knew it would be . . . interesting, before I left Seattle. But I wanted so badly to move closer to home. Not exactly where I grew up, just closer. Glastonbury is perfect for me."

They split up once they got back downtown and each headed home.

Clare got home and sank down on her couch with a bowl of tomato and cheese soup. It was tea time.

Only then did she realize she'd forgotten to check in with Jenny and Marcella to see if they'd found anything amiss when they opened today.

Well, she'd be there tomorrow to find out.

Chapter 6 ～ Skye

Two days later, Skye was in her cozy room at the Sacred Space, giving a massage to Emma. She wore loose light blue rayon trousers and a rayon shirt in the same color. Her feet were bare. The better to feel the energy flowing up from the earth. She'd tied her long hair back in a low ponytail.

The room was warm. Skye felt thirsty, even though she'd been drinking water all morning. No water tasted like that of Faerie, or was as thirst quenching. And being inside a human body messed Skye up completely.

She returned her attention to Emma.

The poor woman was a bundle of knots from spending so much time sewing, hour after hour. Always in the same position.

Jenny had given Skye an oil diffuser as a grand opening gift. Skye had put sage oil in it to purify the room. The scent filled the air, reminding her of countless years of turkey dressing she'd had while living in the States.

The energy surrounding Emma still felt off kilter. She lay naked, belly down on the table, her face in the face rest. A sheet covered her to the waist.

The effect was that Skye felt it difficult to access her own energy. Especially since she was stuck doing all this in a human body. Even though her senses were keener than most humans and the energy flow was too.

It just wasn't good enough for her expectations.

But most people seemed pleased with the work. Raven, Miranda and Jenny had all made paying appointments for next week.

"That's the best massage I've *ever* had," Miranda had said when she left yesterday.

Still, Skye felt the strangeness that had overtaken both the Fae and human worlds since Egan had taken over and imprisoned the Fomorians. It wasn't peaceful. It reminded her of the emptiness of the sea bed before a tsunami.

The drumming music on Skye's player wasn't working for her either. It made her too zoned out. She'd gone five minutes past the end time.

Skye worked on finishing up. Calming the energy down and smoothing things over.

A few minutes later, she said, "When you feel ready, you can sit up and get dressed. Take your time."

"Mmph," said Emma, clearly relaxed. Possibly waking up.

People often drifted off to sleep with her work, especially if they'd been under a lot of stress. Their bodies needed the deep rest.

Skye left the room and went to the loo to wash the oil off her hands. She visualized the excess energy washing down the drain.

She dried her hands and went into the office. Clare was sitting at her computer, frowning.

"Sorry I'm late. You still up for curry?"

"Yes. Anything to knock these numbers out of my head."

"Bad numbers?" asked Skye.

"No, just normal accounting. When I make more money it's the first thing I'm hiring out. Before I hire another person for the store. Not my favorite thing." Clare rubbed her eyes.

The door to the massage room opened and Skye peered out of the office. Emma was emerging. She closed the door behind her and walked towards Skye, smiling.

"Oh my goodness, you *are* gifted. I'll be back and I'm telling all my friends. Thank you so much. I have never, ever had a massage that perfect."

"You're welcome," said Skye. "It was my pleasure."

Emma said to Clare, "She is so wonderful."

"I know," said Clare. "I'm going to have to get a second job just to pay for massages."

Skye's face felt hot. "You're not going back to work are you?" she asked Emma.

Emma said, "No, Miranda warned me that I should plan on taking the rest of the day off. I'm ahead on my sewing schedule, so I'm going home to lie around and read."

"Perfect," said Skye.

After Emma was gone, Clare leaned back in her chair and said, "I've got a problem. I haven't wanted to tell you this, I thought it would be easily solved. But that hasn't happened. Someone's getting into the store and moving things around. I don't know who it is. I'm sure it's not my staff. But I can't figure out how they're getting in."

"What do you mean 'moving things around'?" asked Skye.

"Well, there's the trail of water, it began the morning before you first came in the store. It begins in the back room, just past the hallway and goes into your room. I don't know if it's connected or not. Someone is taking crystals out of the cases and setting them up in your room, as if for a ritual. Plus this appeared and it's not one of ours," said Clare, holding up the fist-sized chunk of opal sitting on her desk.

"Let me see," said Skye, holding her hand out.

Clare handed her the opal. It was lumpy and smooth at the same time, heavy and about the size of a plum. Large compared to most opals she'd seen. The base color was a brownish yellow, but the blue was what stood out.

Skye closed her eyes and searched the opal's energy field. Everyone in the store had handled it. But there was also the trail of someone else.

Dark, heavy and ancient. Primeval. It felt watery, fluid. Skye didn't feel malice, more like confusion and desperation.

That's why the energy in her room felt so weird every morning.

"Whoever this belongs to is confused. They don't mean harm, although that doesn't mean harm won't happen, just that it would be a side effect. This being is ancient."

"Being?" asked Clare, looking alarmed.

"Being," said Skye. "I'm not trying to frighten you. I think it's just searching for someone and your space is a safe haven at the moment."

"Is it here right now?"

"No. I would have sensed it."

"I don't understand. They're getting past the alarm system. I checked with the company and it's working. I called Jimmy, my handyman. He checked the roof and there's no leaks. So I can only guess that this being is pouring water on the floor. So changing the locks isn't going to help?"

"It's not human, I sense a wateriness about it, but I don't know what it is. I'd just leave the crystals where you find them next time."

"What about video cameras?" asked Clare.

"You really are afraid. The cameras might pick it up. Sometimes ethereal beings show up on cameras, other times not. What would that tell you? Do you think you would recognize it?"

"No, but I am afraid. I feel violated."

"I don't know if it means to hurt anyone. It comes at night right? When the store's deserted, no one's around."

Clare nodded. Her face was white with tension.

"That sounds like its avoiding people."

"Is it a ghost?" asked Clare

Marcella had come into the back room and was standing in the doorway.

Marcella said, "What? Our burglar? No, doesn't feel like a ghost."

"How do you know?" asked Clare.

"Ghosts leave a place with a different feeling," Marcella said. "I used to see a lot of ghosts when I was younger. Now, not so much. Anyway, I've never encountered a ghost who burns things."

"Burns things?" asked Skye, the skin on the back of her neck prickling.

"Yeah," said Marcella. "Our burglar likes to burn Nag Champa."

"The incense?"

"Yeah."

"Where? In the same place where it leaves the stones?"

"It burns the incense out in the holder on the front counter," said Marcella.

"It leaves the stones in your room," said Clare, quietly. "It breaks into your room. Pushes the massage table off to the side of the room. I've been pushing it back and picking up the stones when I open in the morning, mopping up. Then locking your door again."

"Is my door locked when you get here?"

"Yes," said Clare.

"Interesting," said Skye. "And it's always the same incense?"

"Yes. What is it?" asked Clare.

"I'm not sure. But for now, why don't you just leave things where it leaves them? See what happens. I'll move my massage table back to where the being puts it when I'm done for the day."

Clare shivered.

Skye put a hand on Clare's shoulder and said, "It'll be all right."

"How do you know that?" asked Clare. "You don't even know what it is."

"Most beings have little interest in the human world. Sometimes they just overlap this one, but they avoid it when they can."

"I hope this one goes away soon," said Clare. "I'm not leaving the water on the floor. It'll ruin the wood."

"Perhaps it will go soon," said Skye.

Skye had no idea what the being was. She'd never encountered anything this old. Except the Fomorians. Had Egan and Meredith missed one when they imprisoned the others? Or was this something completely different? She shuddered at the thought of a Fomorian still wandering around.

What would it do once it located the others? Found them trapped in a vault beneath Faerie.

That evening, at in her room at the boarding house, she waited. When darkness came, Skye took a deep breath and unsealed her human body at the head, neck and shoulders, then slid out of it like a jumpsuit. She was slick all over, which helped keep her Fae body healthy and alive encased inside the human one. She unfolded and fluttered her wings, flattened for days, drying them. Stretching them out.

It felt glorious to be herself again. Her senses reeled, taking in the scent of lavender from her nightstand, hearing the sounds of people in the common room, nearly tasting the tomato sauce from the pizza they were eating and the air touching her bluish Fae skin. The objects in her room had visible auras, a crow feather picked up on a walk surrounded by yellow light. A piece of marble a client had given her held a green aura.

Skye left her human body snuggled cozily in the soft bed and blankets. She opened her bedroom window and climbed naked through it into the tree, feeling the cool air on her skin. Making her feel more vibrant than she had in days. She pulled the window mostly closed, keeping a large rock on the sill so the window couldn't lock shut.

Skye crouched on one of the larger branches. The oak still had its leaves, no one could see her. The cold air felt perfect on her skin and made her tingle all over. She felt so alive being in her own body again. She shook herself to get all the kinks out and extended her long wings again.

Two people were standing on the porch below, snogging. Finally, they stopped. The man left. The woman, who Skye recognized as renting a room downstairs, went inside. After the man drove off, Skye waited a few more minutes.

She straightened quickly and let that momentum shoot her out of the tree before she began moving her wings to gain height and speed.

Skye flew out over the surrounding village and farmland, higher and higher. Thrilling to the wind rushing past her face. The waxing moon had risen and gave her enough light to see perfectly. The area was mostly asleep, but there were some lit up house windows, a few cars driving past.

She flew in larger and larger circles, looking for anything that might give her a clue as to why her energy felt so off. It wasn't only the human body that sensed it. Things felt off to her Fae self too.

It had been thousands of years since she'd been in this area in her sylph body. The coastlines had changed. The surrounding area had been drained hundreds of years ago.

Yet, the sea appeared to be taking it back. Was it the melting of the polar ice caps? The water would eventually swallow large parts of the U.K.

She could feel an eagerness on the part of the sea. A desire to conquer more land. Skye swooped down close enough to feel the icy spray on her face.

The sea was alive still, even though they'd imprisoned Domnu. Or had they? Was it possible to truly contain the Abyss that was the Sea?

Meredith was an elder. A water spirit. She'd seemed to think it was done.

Skye had her doubts. That was the role of air spirits. To think deeply and ask questions that no one wanted to hear.

And the missing air elementals, where had they gone? She'd felt the absence of other sylphs since just after Egan was chosen as Luminary.

She flew for what must have been hours. Searching for answers that never came.

Skye was only left with more questions.

Chapter 7 ❦ Clare

Three days later, Clare stood unlocking the door of the shop, a fluffy black and white tuxedo cat whirling around her feet, mewing.

"Well, hello. Who are you?"

The cat mewed back at her. It was gangly and thin, a teenager who wasn't eating enough.

Clare rubbed the cat's head, then straightened to open the door. She petted it, the fur was surprisingly coarse and wet from the rain. Clare tried to push the cat away as she moved inside the door, but the cat rushed inside before she could close the door. She shut and locked the door.

"Oh, come back here you," she said to the cat.

The cat wasn't paying attention. It roamed around the store, quickly sniffing at things, then moving along and sniffing again.

All Clare could smell was the vanilla and sandalwood scent of Nag Champa. Why did the being choose that one of all the incense in the store? It was a nice scent, one in high demand from her shoppers who used while meditating. The why of it niggled at her though.

Clare went into the back to turn off the alarm system. Switched on the lights in the back and keyed in the pin numbers for the alarm. Then hung her purse on a hook in the back room.

It was cold in the shop this morning, so she turned the heat on before taking off her wool coat and hanging it up.

The trail of water began in the same place in the back room and led to the front, to the crystal case and back to Skye's room.

Curiosity got the better of her and she unlocked Skye's room, switched on the light and peered inside. The crystals and opal were back in the same places they'd been before. And the larger puddle of water sat, probably where the being had lingered.

Clare shut the door. She didn't know what to do. If the being wasn't human, like Skye suggested, then how did one discourage it from coming here? The sense of violation weighed her down.

She glanced at the clock. Almost time to open. Clare switched on the sound system, putting on some Loreena McKennitt. Soothing and invigorating all at the same time.

She got the mop out and quickly cleaned up the front of the store and the back room and the water in Skye's room. She really didn't want the floor ruined. A crusty rim had formed around all the pools as if the water was heavy with minerals.

She got the water heating in the kettle and poured lemongrass green tea into the pot. The lemony scent made her mouth water.

Clare moved on to fill the cash register with money from the bank. Turning the front lights on and unlocking the door, she began to look for the cat.

Just as a group of tourists came in, Clare spotted the cat. It was curled up on the wood floor in front of the radiator, over near the books on shamanism. Sleeping.

The cat was so cute. Four little white paws with a white chin, chest and belly. Most adorable, it had a white exclamation mark between its eyes with the dot on its nose.

Poor thing, it must be really cold being out all night, especially being wet. Well, she'd let the cat warm up, then shoo it out later after the day warmed up a bit. It didn't have a collar. Was it homeless?

Jenny came in not long after the tourists. Her cheeks red, flushed from running probably.

Jenny was always late. A life crammed full of doing too much.

Clare had spent most of her life like that. First working while finishing secondary school. Then holding down two jobs, trying to keep her younger sisters and her alcoholic parents solvent. Then giving up on her parents and earning money to keep her sisters in school, until they married far too young. Then she'd worked two jobs to earn money for her own shop. For years and years.

And to avoid her own non-existent life.

When she'd bought the shop and moved here six months ago, Clare found more spare time than she'd had in her entire life. And she liked it.

She'd never go back to that awfulness of being late for everything because she was over-scheduled.

Jenny said, "Oh, what a cute little cat."

She petted the cat, who mewed at her and allowed itself to be picked up.

"Wow, it's just drugged from the heat. Is it yours?"

"It slipped into the shop when I opened up this morning. Settled down by the heat and I decided to let the poor thing warm up. I don't know who it belongs to."

"It's cute. Look at this beautiful white face with the exclamation point."

Jenny rolled the cat over in her arms. It flopped listlessly, still warm from the radiator. It looked tiny, dwarfed by Jenny's round body. Clare could hear the cat purring across the room.

"Look, she's got a black heart under her chin. And it's a girl. I'll bet she's pregnant."

"No," said Clare, shaking her head. She knew how this scenario went. She didn't want a pet or anyone she had to take care of. And certainly not kittens.

She looked at the cat in Jenny's arms. In the center of its white chin was a perfectly shaped black heart.

"Maybe not, but she sure is skinny. At lunch I'll run over to the pet store and get some food. I'll take a photo of her and ask if they know her, but I'd bet she's a stray."

"Maybe you could take her home. Add her to your collection."

"No. Guinevere would throw a fit. She hates other female cats. Been there, done that."

"Maybe Marcella…"

"No, she has two huge dogs. Lovely girl, but she's so not a cat person."

"Well, hopefully someone will come forward."

"Why can't she live here?" asked Jenny.

"I don't know. What about our night visitor?"

"Maybe it likes cats."

"Maybe it eats cats."

"You're right, we don't know. Maybe Skye could tell us."

Another wave of customers came in, this group completely drenched. The skies had opened up outside.

Jenny put the cat back down by the radiator and went to tidy up around the shop. She rearranged the crystals so there weren't big spaces where the missing ones had been.

Clare went into the back room and began to reconfigure the space in her mind. When the store was empty this afternoon, perhaps Jenny, Marcella and herself could move some shelves around. When Skye was between clients. Clare had a feeling that those opportunities would grow less and less as word about her abilities spread.

Everywhere she went, people were asking about Skye and whether she had openings. She already had a following. Soon, she'd be booked solid. She really was extraordinary.

Clare wanted to get the shelves rearranged before her holiday orders began coming in. Then the shelves would be so packed that they couldn't be moved without unloading everything.

But at least there was a space large enough to hold the rituals and other events. Time was growing short till the first one.

If they could get the shelves all moved around this afternoon, then Friday or Saturday they could hang fabric to drape on the walls. Which she had yet to buy. Time was running out. The ritual was this weekend.

Marcella was opening the store on Friday. And Kristin had said she'd be happy to take Clare shopping for the fabric. So Friday morning then. It was going to take a lot of fabric.

She'd call Kristin after lunch and make arrangements.

Skye came in and she too, oohed and aahed over the cat. Marcella was already trying out names. At lunch Jenny got cat food, bowls, a litter box, a cat bed and other supplies.

"Jonathon said the cat's been hanging around everywhere, looking for a home. For about two weeks now. She's a stray. He's been feeding her now and then, thinks she might be pregnant. But they have too many dogs coming into the pet shop and she's afraid of them. He doesn't want her, doesn't think she'll adapt to the dogs."

Clare sighed.

Maybe it would be good to have a shop cat. Kittens she wasn't sure about.

"Here," said Jenny, handing Clare the can and opener. "You need to feed her. You're the responsible person here. This is really good food. Clean food. Grain free, no preservatives or other crap. This skinny girl needs a good diet, preggers or not."

Clare opened the can and the cat, hearing the can opener, shot towards her from the front room.

"So, she's not wild. She knows that sound," said Jenny.

The cat meowed piteously and rubbed circles round her legs as Clare filled the bowl Jenny had just bought and washed. Clare put the bowl down on the floor, just outside the office.

Jenny filled the other clean bowl with water and set it nearby. Then she filled the cat box with litter and set it around the corner in the back room.

They stood and watched as the cat completely cleaned the bowl of food.

"She was hungry," said Jenny. She picked the cat up and carried her to the litter box.

"This is what mother cats do. They take their kittens to a place to go to the loo as soon as they've nursed. That's how the kids learn."

The cat obviously knew what the litter box was for.

"Well, that's good," said Clare.

"Yeah. You should get her looked over by a vet soon."

"I work nearly every day," said Clare.

"I could come get her tomorrow morning, take her to my vet."

"Okay, if you can take her, I'll pay for the exam, shots and neutering if she's not pregnant."

"Okay. I'll call my vet and see when they can get her in."

The cat sat and bathed for quite a while, then ambled back out to the front and curled up in her new bed next to the heater for most of the afternoon.

Skye did two massage sessions and then went to get lunch. She was off to the chip shop again and took orders for everyone else.

The store was empty, so Clare, Jenny and Marcella went into the back and moved the shelves around.

It took an hour to get everything in the right spot. Marcella kept having to go out front to check for customers. They were making so much noise, no one could hear the bell on the door ring.

Finally, they had one set of wooden shelves lining the other side of the back office wall and the another row in front of the first shelf with only four feet between the rows to form a long aisle. Just enough room to carry a big box down the aisle. Or for two people to be there, unpacking or getting out new stock.

They moved the other shelves so they formed a wall just past Skye's room and set up another aisle in front of the first shelves with the remaining shelves.

Everything was dusty and they were all sneezing.

"I'll vacuum after lunch," said Jenny.

"I'll dust first," said Marcella. "I didn't know a place could get so dusty."

They would be able to drape fabric on the back of the rows of shelving and use them as a boundary for the event space. The other two boundary walls were formed by the back left corner of the building. All together it formed a nice large square in the back corner. About twice as large as the shop out front. And empty.

She'd get some fancy braided curtain cords to close off the ends of the aisles during events so people wouldn't wander through the back stock.

Clare brushed off her peach-colored blouse and tan trousers, trying to get the dust off. Then fluffed out her hair, hoping it helped remove some dust.

By that time Skye was back with lunch.

Clare washed her hands and face, drying them with the rough paper towel. The white paper still came away brown. It took two washings to get everything off. How had the back room gotten so dirty in only six months?

The cat followed Skye into the office, her nose twitching. Clare dished up more cat food for her and she ate happily.

The four of them sat in the office and ate the fish and chips. The smell of fish and fat filled the air. The fish tasted rich and greasy. Clare put tartar on hers, but she could smell the vinegar from Marcella's lunch. It tickled her nose.

She licked her fingers.

"You all are filthy," said Skye, "but the place looks great."

"I really like it. I think it'll be perfect for events," said Jenny.

"We just need to clean it thoroughly and decorate," said Clare.

"Ooh when?" asked Marcella.

"Cleaning, this afternoon. We'll decorate once I've gotten the fabric and lights," said Clare.

Skye said, "I never realized how big the space is. The back's much larger than the front."

"Huge," said Clare.

"Larger than the twenty people you put a cap on for the ritual."

"I know," said Clare. "I wanted to start smaller. See how it all worked out."

"And all those shelves are nearly empty," said Skye.

"Just wait. We've got oodles of stuff coming in for the holidays. I've been letting things get low back here to make room for holiday storage. I wanted to sell out all the old stock first."

"Good thing," snorted Jenny. "Otherwise we would have had to move ten million books along with the shelves. And that would've taken us another week."

Clare reveled in the fat and fish flavor mingling with the tartar sauce. Glorious. She really did need to splurge on going out more often. Bringing her own lunch all the time had gotten really boring. Healthier, but boring.

The cat, having finished her meal, jumped up on an empty wooden chair and began bathing. As if she knew everyone, trusted them and was just one of the gang. As if she belonged there.

"Wow, she's comfortable," said Jenny. "She'll be a really good shop cat. Sociable."

Skye nodded.

"What about our night visitor?" asked Clare.

"What?" asked Skye.

"She's afraid it will eat the cat," said Jenny.

"Eew," said Marcella.

"I don't think so," said Skye, closing her eyes. "It's not really in our world. I mean, it picks up the crystals and moves them. But it's not…"

"Corporeal?" asked Marcella.

"Exactly. It's not fully here. I don't know if it can be."

"So, the cat's safe here?" asked Clare.

"See you do care about her," said Jenny.

"I want her to be safe."

"I think she'll be fine here," said Skye. "If she feels threatened, she'll hide. Give her some hiding spaces."

Everywhere's a hiding space around here," said Clare.

The bell rang as the front door opened. Marcella had finished her lunch, so she went to wash up and go out front. Jenny finished soon after.

Skye hurried through her lunch, she had a client coming.

"I've got a break at two if you want to vacuum then."

"Great, I'll have Marcella dust quietly until then."

After lunch, Clare called Kristin and arranged to go fabric shopping on Friday morning.

Chapter 8 ❦ Skye

Skye mopped up the floor in her massage room again the next morning. Her room looked the same as always, except the massage table was pushed to one side, the group of stones she'd put outside the door of her room and the pool of water. There was more water every day. The scent of Nag Champa lingered in the air even back here. It even overpowered the rose oil that she'd used yesterday afternoon with her last client.

She carried the mop and bucket into the bathroom and rinsed them in the sink, squeezing the mop out a couple of times. Then she wiped out the sink with a paper towel and put the damp mop and bucket back in the cleaning cupboard.

Skye washed her hands in the bathroom sink. Then smoothed her hair, and adjusted the sage green leggings and spring green tunic.

She walked across the wood floor to her room in her bare feet, avoiding the still damp spots.

Skye felt relieved she'd gotten there early enough to clean up before her client arrived. It was the second week that the being had used her room and it bothered her more than she let the others know.

Skye couldn't be sure if it meant harm to her or the other staff, but most annoying, she couldn't figure out what the being was. Until that became clear she couldn't understand what it was doing here and why it lingered.

Skye felt a rush of tension surge through her. Soon, someone from Faerie would come and want to know what she had accomplished. How close she was to making contact, coming out as Fae.

She felt as if this would take an eternity. Faerie didn't have an eternity. The human world would begin to stumble across Faerie, probably sooner rather than later.

There was a lot of chatter in the front of the store. Another clutch of customers had just come in the door. Must be tourists. They always seemed to travel in packs.

Skye picked up the four crystals and the opal, and took them to one of the recently rearranged shelves in back. She set them on an empty shelf, feeling an almost ominous vibration from the opal. Staring at the opal, Skye picked it up again. She held it with her eyes closed, trying to sense everything about it. Shocked, she set it back on the shelf again and rubbed her hands together to dispel the feel of it. The stone felt dark, darker than an opal should. Skye nervously pushed strands of hair from her face and went back to her room.

She closed her door, locked it and moved the massage table back to the center of the room, switching the heater on. Then rummaging around in her drawer, Skye closed her eyes and asked which incense to use today. Amber. She should use amber.

She pulled the incense out and struck a match, lighting it and watching the smoke whirl around. She walked around her room clearing and cleansing the space.

Skye pushed her panic into a darkened room in her mind.

She must make this space peaceful and serene for her clients who needed to feel safe in order to heal. And she had to find the clarity to do her work.

Wrestling with her feelings about the being would have to wait till later.

Skye set the incense in its holder. Then put a clean sheet on the massage table and turned on the warming pad for it. She tidied up and made sure everything was in its right place and switched on some soft Celtic music, slow airs.

The ritual of doing ordinary things usually served to calm and center her.

She switched on the two dim lamps, turned off the overhead and slipped into her clogs. Then she went out and closed the door.

Skye walked out front, waved to Jenny who stood at the cash register and said, "I'll be right back. If my client gets here while I'm gone, tell her to go on in."

Jenny nodded, a surprised look on her face, then answered the ringing phone.

Skye walked out of the shop and into the crisp fall breeze. She moved briskly down the mostly empty sidewalk, breathing deeply. Taking in the air.

It was too cold out for wearing just a tunic and leggings, but she hadn't thought about grabbing a jacket.

She went round the entire block, shaking her arms, trying to clear out the strange being's energy. By the time she'd reached the store again, she'd calmed herself enough to work.

She entered the store at the same time as her client. A new client, Sarah, who was dressed in a white tailored shirt, black trousers and heels. On top she wore a black suit coat and looked very businesslike. Not like someone who'd just popped out for a massage.

"Hi," said Skye. "I'll take you back."

She led Sarah to the massage room and opened the door. The tall, thin woman looked pinched and pale. She was probably in her forties. Successful, but going through hard times Skye guessed.

"Oh, I love the incense," said Sarah.

"Good."

Skye usually left the door open while burning incense. It tended to be a little overpowering. But she hadn't thought. Hadn't been sure how long she'd be outside and knew she had to warm up the room.

She left the door open for a bit, to shoo out some of the smoke, while they sat and talked. Skye did her usual spiel about how she worked. Asked Sarah if there was anything in particular that she wanted to work on.

Sarah gave a deep sigh.

"I'm getting a divorce. It feels like it's been going on forever, but I know from watching my friends' experiences that it's just beginning and our daughter just left home for the first time. I'm all alone and trying to make decisions."

"So, you're hurting and trying to find clarity all at once," said Skye.

Sarah laughed. "Yes. I went to see Raven the other day. She said that she'd just gotten a massage from you and that I needed to do a lot of self care right now. I've never had a massage before, but then I'd never had a tarot reading either, and that turned out to be quite lovely."

"Okay, well let's see what I can do. I'll leave for a few minutes. You can undress, hang your clothes on the hooks if you like and get on the table under the sheet. Do you like heat?"

"Heat feels wonderful these days. It's getting so cold out."

"I'll leave the massage table warmer on then."

"Should I take off my undies?"

"I'll leave that up to what makes you comfortable. You'll need to take your bra off."

Skye stood and left the room.

She went to just inside the back room where she'd left a cup of tea brewing before she cleaned up her room. The tea was still a little warm. She sipped it.

Jenny came back and said, "Are you all right?"

"I'm fine. I just needed to get some air. Clear out my energy."

"It's the being, isn't it? The energy is getting stronger."

"You can feel it?"

Skye hadn't thought of Jenny as particularly sensitive.

"Yeah, and I don't like it."

Skye said, "Well, I can't talk about it right now. I need to be clear enough to do my work. Maybe at lunch? I don't have any appointments this afternoon, so it won't matter."

"Great. Shall I invite Clare and Marcella?"

"Maybe not yet. Clare's completely freaked out about it already."

"Okay. Want to go for curry?"

"That sounds lovely."

Jenny went back out front to help customers. Skye drank her tea for several minutes and tried to tune into her client's needs.

Then she washed her hands again, out of habit, and went in to work.

Skye had two more clients before she broke for lunch. It was a good beginning to her first week of paying customers.

Skye and Jenny walked through the rain to the Indian restaurant. She still hadn't gotten a raincoat and water seeped in through her heavy wool jumper, which smelled like wet dog.

Jenny opened the door and Skye could almost feel the wall of spices hit her nose. Cardamon, cumin and mustard seeds were the first she could identify. Her mouth began to water.

They sat at one of the empty wooden tables and picked up the menus.

Skye quickly decided on garlic naan and chicken in a coconut sauce and tea.

After they'd ordered Jenny asked, "Well, what do you think?"

"About the being?"

Jenny nodded and poured tea for them from the plain white teapot.

"I don't know what to think, but its presence is getting stronger and more disturbing. I really thought it would have moved on by now," said Skye.

"Do you think it will hurt us?" asked Jenny.

"I don't know."

"Pirate didn't seem to be bothered when I arrived this morning."

"Pirate?"

Jenny said, "We're trying out that name for the cat. The black heart under her chin looks piratey."

"She probably feels safer in the warm store with places to hide than out on the street with cars and stray dogs. And people who hate cats."

"I'm not sure I would. This being, whatever it is, gives me the willies."

Their food came and Skye dipped the soft flatbread into the sauce for the chicken and bit into it. The coconut and cream flavors unfolded in her mouth, followed by the garlic and curry. She smiled at the rich decadence of it.

"Good?" asked Jenny, before taking a bite of her chicken marsala.

"Amazing."

Jenny nodded.

"What does the being's energy feel like to you?" asked Skye.

Jenny swallowed and said, "I've never felt anything like this thing. I don't understand why there's always water because the energy feels big and heavy. Full of sorrow. Like a lost giant child that can't find its mother. It doesn't feel mature. I don't know why. But that's what I get."

"Do you 'get' feelings like this often?"

"I do. Mostly it's about what people are going through. I've got enough psychic powers to pick up vibes from people.

Not enough that I feel comfortable being a Psychic. Not for a living. I wouldn't want that responsibility. It's easier to just give my opinion now and again, when people ask my advice about their lives."

"Well, being a mom's a full time job."

"No kidding. So, what about you? How do you feel about this being? What do you think it is?"

"I really don't know. I do know it's old. It may act like a child, but it's ancient. Searching for something. Using the opal mainly, but also the incense."

"And where did the opal come from?"

"The being brought it with it."

"So why the water? Is it from the sea?" asked Jenny.

"It's sea water that it drips."

"Really? How can you tell?"

"I tasted it. It's quite salty. And smells like the sea."

"You can smell it in that small amount of water?"

"I have a fabulous nose. If I wasn't doing massage, I could work for a perfumer."

"So, we have an ancient sea being, who's come on land, bringing a chunk of opal with it and searching for what?" asked Jenny.

"I don't know," said Skye, sipping the hot, strong tea.

"Nag Champa is used for meditation and purification. It contains sandalwood, so it's got a watery aspect to it. What is our friend looking for?"

"You're right about the sense of sorrow. I get that too but I don't know what it's looking for. Others of its kind? A mother, like you said? Something it lost or escaped from it? I've got nothing."

Jenny asked, "Is it attracted to all the ley lines?"

"The what?" asked Skye.

"Ley lines, you know lines of energy. Glastonbury is sort of a center where many, many ley lines converge. You should look at the maps sometime."

"I didn't know that. I just felt the energy is really strong here. Easy to tap into for healing." Skye hadn't known that many humans were aware of the energy, let alone mapped it.

"Okay, well do you think there's something we should or could do for it? To help it move along?"

"If I knew what it was or what it wanted, I might have an answer to that question." Skye wished she did. Thinking about the being made the muscles in her human body constrict. Fear. That was what she'd been fighting every time she'd cleaned up the water. Now the scent of Nag Champa had become associated with the being in her mind. She'd probably never burn it again.

Jenny nodded. "Maybe we should ask Raven."

"You think she'd know?" Raven wouldn't know what it was.

"She's incredibly sensitive. More than me. She might be able to give us some more information."

"I don't know how Clare would feel about that."

"I don't either, but I can tell you that we're quickly coming up on the Samhain ritual and I don't know what time after closing this being shows up, but I'm not sure it would be helpful to have it show up in the evening of that event."

Skye leaned back in her chair and said, "I hadn't thought of that."

"Let me talk to Clare, see if I can get her okay to share this. She doesn't know Raven well, but I'll see what I can do to talk her round. We need to try something."

"You're right. I wasn't even thinking about Samhain."

A niggling thought rose up inside her. Skye pushed it down. She'd think about it later. When she was alone.

They finished lunch and walked back to the store.

Skye went into the back, picked up the chunk of opal off the shelf, went into her room and shut the door. And locked it.

She lit a couple of candles, then sat on the floor in the middle of the room, holding the opal.

She let go of the physical world, cradling the opal in both of her human hands. Letting her sylph mind move out of the human body, she let it slip between the floor boards in the back room, following the trail of the being. Skye found a hollow beneath the building, a tunnel made long ago. It smelled of damp earth. She moved quickly down the narrow tunnel, crawling, wings folded tight to her body. There were numerous large stones lying on the tunnel floor, football size. She kept banging into them with her feet and hands, even though her physical body was still back in her room. The rocks were sharp, as if the tunnel hadn't been naturally eroded, but chiseled out by someone, possibly humans.

The soil was damp and she heard a roaring sound in front of her. Water, flowing swiftly. An underground stream. The tunnel ended at the water. It looked about five feet across, but she could see no opening on the other side of the stream. She sensed the being had simply moved into the water, its trail faded quickly. Skye followed. She let herself be tossed by the water. The river let out into the ocean. She felt herself sink, following the being back to depths. Even through the water, she could sense him.

Him, the being was a him.

Skye was insignificant, invisible in this alien world of the ocean. She let herself sink deeper and deeper and found him sulking in the bottom of the abyss.

Then suddenly, she panicked and found herself thrust back into her sylph and human bodies.

She dropped the opal, watching it crack into several pieces.

Skye wrapped her arms around her legs, put her head down and rocked.

It was impossible.

Absolutely impossible.

Chapter 9 ❦ Clare

Clare stood on the second to the top step of the tall ladder in the back room. She used a strip of material to anchor the gauzy, scarlet fabric to the wall hook. Draping it a bit lower and to the right, she tied it to another metal hook that she'd put up yesterday.

Letting go of the fabric, she climbed down the tall wood ladder. One hand on the rough wall to steady herself, even though there was nothing to hang onto except the flimsy fabric. The ladder wobbled with each step down that she took. It almost made her heart stop with fear, even though the ladder didn't fall over.

She hated this part of the decorating. Hated ladders and heights.

But Marcella was up front, busy with a regular customer who loved her and always bought things.

And this needed to get done.

Samhain was tomorrow night. Tomorrow afternoon, Kristin and Raven were coming in to bring their decorations and set things up. The walls needed to be done.

Marcella and Jenny had vacuumed and dusted, then mopped. The back room was spotless, with no dust to make her sneeze. That was good at least.

Since Clare had returned with the fabric, she'd been burning sage in the back room. Trying to get rid of the smell of cleaning chemicals and Nag Champa. She'd always rather liked the incense, but now it filled her with dread. The sinking feeling she felt every morning when opening the store and knowing once again, that the being had been there.

The sage smoke filled the air, making everything look slightly hazy. But the scent was wonderful, taking her to a different place.

Almost. It didn't dispel all her worries though.

She stood back and looked at her work. She'd put up the lights on both walls and the back of the two bookcases. Then the strips of scarlet gauze over them on two walls so far. She'd do the scarlet on the bookcases next. Next she'd layer on the burnt orange and chocolate brown gauze in rivulets so that each of the colors showed in different places.

She pulled her jeans up and smoothed the purple T-shirt back down. The jeans were getting too loose. She wasn't eating enough.

Marcella came into the back.

"She's gone. What can I do to help?"

"How are you with ladders?"

"I'm good. You know, I've never seen you wear trainers before."

Clare looked down at her shoes. "I rarely wear them. But fancy shoes and ladders," she shivered exaggeratedly and Marcella laughed.

Clare pushed the ladder a few feet to the right, handed Marcella the fabric ties and gestured for Marcella to climb.

"Okay, grab the fabric on the way up and I'll tell you what I want."

Two hours later, they had the three bolts of gauze hung up on the walls and backs of shelves. The large corner of the room was resplendent in scarlet red, burnt orange and a deep, warm brown the color of chocolate.

Clare plugged the clear LED fairy lights into two different surge protectors. The black cords disappeared behind the folds of the fabric. She had tucked the surge protectors against the wall so people wouldn't trip over them, but where they'd still be accessible to turn on and off.

Then she went to the hallway and switched off the overhead lights.

The fairy lights glowed beneath the fabric, making the nearly dark room look magical. It glowed with color.

Marcella had a hand over her mouth. "It's so beautiful."

Pirate sat on a wooden table they'd set in the corner, watching everything. She was fascinated.

Clare went over to the table and picked up her mug of cold tea and sipped it, tasting the black tea and cream. She patted Pirate's now soft fur, remembering how coarse it had been when she'd first arrived at the store.

The cat was growing plumper by the hour. Her coat was looking better and she charmed everyone who came in the store. Clare loved how the cat followed her around, sitting on her lap when she was working in the office. Pirate spent her time mostly eating or sleeping. The vet guessed she had about a week to go before she gave birth. They'd made her a cozy covered bed in the office. And locked her in there at night to keep her safe.

Clare didn't want her to be anywhere near the being when it came.

She didn't want to think about the being. She'd spent the last two evenings here, till midnight, putting in orders and working on the events schedule.

The thing hadn't shown up until after she left. She hoped that it would stay away until after the ritual was over tomorrow night.

She shivered. The thought of it still creeped her out.

Skye was supposed to come back today. She'd gone over to Ireland for a two day break. Clare had missed her and was glad she'd be here tomorrow night. She felt nervous about the ritual even though she wasn't leading it, simply providing the space.

Clare and Marcella rolled out four huge woven mats over the floor in the ritual space. She and Kristin had gotten them at a garden center. They'd be better for people to sit on tomorrow night than the cold wood floor. And the tan mats worked with the color theme.

Clare had planned out the decor for the eight major celebrations so there'd be some overlap. She'd reuse the scarlet fabric for the Winter Solstice or Yule ritual, adding white and a deep green. Then for Imbolc in February she'd reuse the white. She'd gotten mats in four different colors and planned to use each one twice during the year.

It was a good thing she'd been keeping a large chunk of money in savings. With Skye paying rent she'd have a little extra to tuck away for future expenses.

The bells on the front door rang and Marcella went out front.

Clare went back over to the table in the corner and petted Pirate. The cat climbed into her arms and began purring.

"What do you think, honey? It's gorgeous isn't it?"

The cat meowed in response.

"I think it'll be a very nice ritual."

Marcella returned to the back of the store, followed by Jenny.

"Wow, this is awesome!" Jenny stroked Pirate's ears and the cat closed her eyes in bliss.

"What are you doing today?" asked Clare.

"I was running errands and I just had to see how it was coming along. It looks spectacular."

"It does, doesn't it," said Clare.

"I love it. And I think it'll be perfect for tomorrow," said Marcella.

"Are you two coming?" asked Clare.
"Wouldn't miss it," said Jenny.
"Me either," said Marcella.
"Good. If I need help out front, I'll pay you if you help out."
"Just let us know when the time comes," said Jenny.
"Okay. I have no idea what to expect," said Clare.
"It'll be fine. Just fine," said Jenny.
"How many people are coming?" asked Marcella.
"Kristin said they've got twelve confirmed, but there might be a couple more. Then there's us and Skye. So at least sixteen. Maybe eighteen. But more people are signed up on the clipboard by the register," Clare said. "Should we take the flyers in the store down?"

"I don't think so," said Marcella. "Even if we're full up, it's good publicity for the next event. Leave it up for a couple more days."

"Good idea," said Clare. "I really do need to take that online marketing course."

"What are you going to do with Pirate?" asked Jenny.

"I'll put her in the office just before the ritual begins. I don't want her to be a distraction."

"I think that's a good idea. She sure is adapting well. She loves the customers and they love her. I've had four people tell me they want one of her kittens. Sight unseen," said Marcella. "They just love her personality so much."

The bell rang again and Marcella went out front. She returned leading a Royal Mail Delivery guy. He rolled a hand cart into the back room and unloaded three very large, heavy boxes next to one of the shelf aisles.

Clare signed for it and got a box knife to open them, switching on the overhead lights so they could see. She took the paperwork out and made sure all the items were there.

"Oh, look at this," squealed Marcella. "I heard she had a new book out," waving a copy of *Glastonbury Unveiled: New Research Linking the Tor, Red Chalice Well and the White Spring*.

"Yay," said Jenny. "Leave one out for me too. I'm so pleased it's finally out."

Clare finished counting books in the first two boxes and then dug into the third box. In amongst the packing were more beautiful crystals and boxes of jewelry. Pendants in separate plastic bags. Rings in their own bags, as were earrings and bracelets.

She took the boxes of jewelry and began unloading them onto empty shelves, spreading them out so she could make sure everything was there. The lighting wasn't great here with the shelves now so close together. She'd have to put better lights up one of these days.

When she was done and everything was accounted for, Clare took a third of the jewelry out front and set it near the cash register for Marcella to put out on display.

Pirate sat by her empty bowl.

"Oh dear, are you out of food again? Those little parasites eating all your food?"

Clare opened a new can and scooped some into her bowl.

She entered the new inventory into the computer. Then came out to find Jenny and Marcella shelving some of the new books out front.

"Hey you, you're not supposed to be working today," said Clare.

"I know. I just don't want to go buy groceries. Really, it's pointless. The food disappears as fast as I can buy it. Do you have any idea how much three growing boys eat?"

Clare laughed.

"I think you need to go out to dinner!" said Marcella.

"I do. Leave all those boys to fend for themselves. I should go and get it done. Before they eat all the ice cream for dinner. Oh wait, they already did that. Gotta restock ice cream," she said, flinging her hands in the air.

Jenny grabbed her coat, purse and the new book. Clare checked out the book, minus her discount, took her debit card and when she was finished Jenny walked towards the front door.

"See you tomorrow."
"Bye," said Marcella.
"Thanks Jenny," said Clare.
Jenny waved and she was gone.

Clare and Marcella got some of the new stock and some of the extra back stock out and displayed before closing. Tomorrow they'd clean up all the empty boxes and packing materials. And do a thorough cleaning before the ritual.

Marcella left and Clare locked the front door. She turned off all the lovely fairy lights in back. Gave Pirate's fresh food and water in the office and emptied the litter box. By that time, Pirate was already back in her bed near the desk, sleeping.

Clare switched on some gentle classical music for her. To muffle whatever sounds the night visitor might make. She liked to think it helped keep Pirate less afraid.

The poor cat had had a rough life so far. The vet said she was barely six months old. Still a baby, and pregnant.

"Good night dear. I'll see you in the morning. Sleep well," she said.

Pirate purred in response, but didn't open her eyes.

Clare locked the office. Checked the back area, then turned out the overhead lights for the back and front. Switched off the music system for the store.

The cash register was already done, so she picked up the bank bag, turned on the alarm system and left, locking the door.

She still felt nervous about tomorrow night.

And Skye hadn't stopped in this afternoon. She was supposed to be back in town around three. Well, maybe she'd been tired and gone straight home.

Clare hoped everything would be all right tomorrow.

After she dropped the bag at the bank, she walked towards home, taking deep breaths and telling herself everything would be fine.

She almost believed it.

Chapter 10 ~ Skye

Skye woke up in her own bed at the boarding house. It was still dark outside. Before dawn. She drank some water and ate cheese and crackers from an instant packet. Giving her human body just enough nourishment for it to sustain itself for a couple of days without her presence. After washing its face, smearing moisturizer on the body and brushing and braiding the long hair, Skye lay down on the still warm bed and slid out of her human body. She arranged it on the pillows and tucked the covers around it.

She walked around the room, feeling her own skin gradually dry. She stretched her wings, fluttering them and letting them loosen and dry off as well. It was always such a relief to be back in her own body, her wings extended. Checking her mobile for messages, Skye turned off the sound and plugged it into the charger.

Then she opened the window, climbed up onto the sill and out into the tree, pulling the window mostly closed behind her, but putting a rock in the crack so it wouldn't lock her out.

Skye flew out of the tree, diving at first, allowing her wings a chance to really stretch before she soared up above the tree line of the village. The air felt cold and crisp to her skin and she smiled with pleasure. She flapped her wings using the full extension of each pulse, surging forward towards the sea, feeling the immense power of flying. It thrilled her.

Coasting on the zephyrs and catching the occasional tail wind helped strengthen her. She always forgot how healing being in her element could be.

Skye knew she was spending too much time in human form. She really should fly every night. Not get sucked into the human body's need for sleep.

She didn't need to sleep so much, the human body did. If she didn't get out before it crashed, then the body's need for sleep dragged her down too.

As she passed over boundary of sea and land, the sun began to rise.

Skye felt the air whipping past her, smelled the kelp and tasted the salt from the sea. Felt the coolness of winter approaching. Her knee length, whitish blond hair streamed behind her, tangling and untangling itself around her hips and legs.

She flew through several clouds and opened her mouth to catch the rainwater. It tasted fresh, quenching her thirst.

Hours later, as she grew closer to Faerie, Skye began to descend. Gulls whirled around her, playing tag. Their shrieking cries a cacophony that was almost deafening.

It only took nine hours to fly to Faerie. It felt much shorter.

On the way, she caught shadows of other sylphs, but only shadows. They weren't fully there, just their spirits. She would have followed, tried to find out what was happening with them, but there was no time right now.

When Skye reached the palace, she circled overhead. It was formed from the trunks of ten living massive pine trees. Woven around the trunks were walls of intertwined willows and vines, a living building as only Fae and nature could have created. The covered vault in front of the building, with the garden planted over it, lay cloaked in fall color and the streaming fountains looked perfect. Inside that vault the Fomorians had been imprisoned. Nothing seemed amiss.

Skye knew it was an illusion.

Something was terribly wrong.

She flew to an opening near the roof of the palace and landed on a ledge made for air spirits. A tall doorway led to the inside of the palace and an interior platform which hung high above the throne room. The huge room was made of the woven living willows and vines with a floor made of stone tiles. Here and there elegant woven tapestries hung, showing some part of Fae history. The woven walls were lined with stained glass windows, an art form humans had stolen from the Fae, yet never mastered. Oil lamps were placed on the walls. The ceiling stood open in several places, allowing smoke from the fire pits to rise and escape, but the foliage above kept most of the rain and snow out.

The room was crowded with Fae, all lined up, patiently waiting their turn as the Luminary, Egan, spoke to them individually.

She didn't have time to wait for him to finish.

Meredith stood to one side, speaking with a group of other elders.

Meredith would know. Skye hoped.

She landed nearby and Meredith saw her.

"My dear child," she said, holding out her arms in welcome.

Skye ran to Meredith and embraced her. Meredith was a water spirit. They all leaked, so Skye came away feeling damp.

"I need to talk quickly and return," she said.

Meredith signaled a kitchen Fae for refreshments. The Fae brought Skye a mug of tea and a plate of sliced beef and cheese, from the farms of Faerie.

"What's wrong?" asked Meredith, her watery face wrinkling up as she turned back to Skye.

Meredith led her out of the throne room and into the gardens behind the palace. Skye ate a slice of the intensely salty, marinated meat as they walked, only just realizing how hungry she was. Once they were in the gardens, they sat on wooden benches beneath bare vines. The yellow leaves lay at their feet like a carpet. The garden preparing for winter.

It was beginning to get cooler out, even during the day. The sun hid behind a layer of thick clouds. Egan obviously wasn't moderating the temperature in Faerie as the previous Luminaries had when she was young. Faerie had always been a place of everlasting summer. Perhaps Egan didn't know how. Or maybe he wanted Faerie to see a full cycle of seasons.

After finishing the meat and sipping her tea made of strong mint and fragrant rosebuds, Skye told Meredith what was happening in Glastonbury.

"And so you think this being is what?" asked Meredith.

"A Fomorian. I'm not sure who. It seems male, but it feels strong and watery like Domnu. Did we really contain her? I mean who can contain the abyss?"

Meredith sighed and looked down.

"I've wrestled and wrestled with that question," she said. "We've seen no signs of her, or of any of them escaping the trap. But we wouldn't would we? Domnu could go down. Out through cracks, into the earth and ultimately back into the sea. The winds would escape through cracks and seep into the air. Their essence might still be trapped though, and they might not be completely whole. I just don't know."

"Does Egan know?"

Meredith shook her head and said, "What should I tell him? That I'm suspicious other things went wrong with the spell than what affected him? Or that it simply might not be possible to cage the Fomorians and their wild elements with any spell?"

Skye sighed.

"So what do we do now?"

"I should come see this creature. And perhaps bring Dylan."

"How long will it take you to get there?" asked Skye. She explained about the upcoming ritual. "I'm afraid when the humans call in the element of water for their ritual that the being will come."

"Not an unfounded fear, I'd say," said Meredith. "You go back. I'll gather who we can and travel the fastest way possible."

"You'll need to be in human bodies if you're coming to the ritual."

"Oh bother. I dislike being human so."

Skye narrowed her eyes.

"Okay, we'll make sure we don't scare your friends."

Skye nodded.

"I'm worried about the other sylphs? Have any of them returned?"

"No," said Meredith. "And Aura is not as strong as she once was. She's worried too, but has no idea where they are."

Skye nodded. The sylph had never been her mentor, but as an elder, Aura would have remained at the palace and not left with the other sylphs. So perhaps they were the only two air spirits left. She pushed the thought aside, along with her feelings. She didn't want to go there right now.

"How are things here?" asked Skye.

"We're still trying to deal with the effects of Faerie being closed so long. The few elders left are either slowly reviving, or dying off. It's tragic. New energy is coming into Faerie. And our magic is moving out into the world. Some humans are slowly finding they can make seemingly magical things happen. Little things like wishing someone's illness away and finding that the person recovers unexpectedly. Lost pets being found. I don't know how this will all end up. Are humans ready for magic?"

"Some of them are. Others won't ever be," said Skye. "but about the Fomorians. Is Egan worried?"

"We all are. None of us know how long the spell will hold or what to do when it fails."

"But you're trying, searching for an answer?" asked Skye.

"Of course we are. That's why finding all the elders is so crucial. I think we will find the answer in the past somewhere. They were the ones who defeated the Fomorians in the first place. The Tuatha de Danann. Our ancestors." Meredith sighed. She looked weary.

"Let me know if I can help," said Skye.

"You're doing enough. You must focus on your task, you, Adaire and the others. I do not know how long Faerie will continue to be open. If there are Fomorians loose and we haven't found a way to contain them . . . I don't want to close Faerie again, but there may be no other way to protect our home. All of you will have to return. I sense war in the air," said Meredith, grimly.

"I will try to make things move faster." Her heart felt heavy.

Skye got up and went back to the throne room to return her plate and mug. She glanced at Egan, still helping Fae. He hadn't even looked up and seen her. Fire elements. They were so intense.

Skye left the palace and took to the air. She flew into the forest and sipped a few lingering honeysuckle flowers for a bit until she felt refreshed.

As the sun was setting, she flew back to Glastonbury.

If she flew straight, and if the wind blew her direction, she could get back by morning. And sleep all day. Waking in time for the ritual.

She saw the shadows of sylphs again. But when she tried to follow, they led her far off course. She headed back and ignored them. They weren't actually sylphs, merely shadows. Could it be a trap? Using the shadows as bait?

But who would set such a trap?

It worried her because she only had one answer to that question. And they should all be contained in the vault in Faerie.

Later in the night, a massive dark cloud followed her. Moving far too close and too fast.

Skye flew lower and landed on the side of a large boat, making herself thin and invisible, folding her wings in. She hung near the back of the vessel. The boat rocked with the huge waves, but it went forward towards England. She was soaked from the sea water but didn't dare fly until the cloud finally left, unable to find her.

Was it now unsafe for her to even fly?

What was happening?

She clung to the side of the boat, her fingers growing numb and frozen. The chill from the wind was something she normally thrived on. But it was becoming more than even she could withstand.

Then the boat turned too far south.

Skye fluttered her wings, getting them warm and limber again. Then she shot off the boat and flew back towards land and Glastonbury. She kept low, hoping to escape notice from the clouds, but high enough the sea couldn't reach her either.

Once on land, she sprinted, staying invisible from humans only because it was night. Still she moved from woodland to woodland, trying to avoid any pattern. Her return trip seemed to take forever.

Skye kept perching in trees, shaking with fear, and waiting for anything that might be following her to appear. She saw nothing.

Finally, she caught sight of the tree outside her window. She flew and landed in it, then climbed down the branch and opened the window. Slipping inside, she closed the window after herself and locked it.

Her room was quite warm. She stood by the radiator, still quivering from fear.

It felt exactly like the time she'd been caught by the Fomorians.

It seemed to take hours before she could stop shaking and make sense of it.

The Fomorians must have escaped. Somehow. And they'd taken all the other sylphs. That's why the air spirits had disappeared.

She didn't understand what the shadows had been. Or if the sylphs were even still alive.

Or how exactly Meredith and Dylan would come to Glastonbury. But if they were swimming, they weren't safe. They'd only be safe if they used human bodies as disguises.

So, they might not make it in time for the ritual. Or at all. She was on her own.

And didn't have any idea how to trap the Fomorian who came every night to Clare's store, or even chase it away.

Eventually, she gave up thinking and slipped back into her human body and oblivion.

Chapter 11 ~ Clare

Clare unlocked the shop and walked inside. It was the last day of October. The Samhain ritual was tonight.

Anticipation mingled with grogginess. She had been so excited last night it had taken a couple of hours of lying in bed just to calm down enough to get to sleep. She desperately needed a cup of strong tea.

Orange twinkle lights hung throughout the store, casting a strange murky purple color on the floor as it mingled with the morning sunshine. The scent of Nag Champa was in the air again. She gave a deep sigh of resignation.

If the being ever did go away, she'd never burn that incense again.

She closed the door behind her and locked it. Then went into the back and switched off the alarm.

Shivering in the cold, Clare turned the heat up higher to get the store warmed up quickly.

As usual there was a trail of water on the floor. Clare turned the lights on and quickly filled the till, getting the store ready to open.

Then she opened the office door. Pirate needed feeding.

The smells of the shut up room, the litter box and fishy cat food greeted her. The office felt nice and warm though. Pirate meowed from her bed, but didn't get up.

Clare switched the light on and said, "Good morning honey."

"Mrow," replied Pirate.

"Oh my," said Clare.

Lying next to Pirate were six kittens in a rainbow of colors. A yellow orange tabby and a solid black were nursing. A solid gray kitten, a white, a gray striped tabby and a tortoiseshell with black, orange and white patches were all curled in a pile, sound asleep.

"What beautiful kittens. What a good kitty you are, having these babies all by yourself. I'll bet you're hungry."

Pirate purred, but didn't get up.

Clare picked up the bowls off their mat in the corner and cleaned them. Then refilled one with fresh water and set it within Pirate's reach. Then she opened a new can of food and spooned some into the other bowl and put it close to the cat as well.

The vet had told them to do that. Also that Pirate would probably eat all the placentas and umbilical cords. Clare looked at the kittens, but didn't touch them. She didn't want to disturb them.

Pirate ate a bit of the wet food, then settled back to sleep.

Clare switched on the desk lamp and turned off the overhead lights. That way there'd be enough light to see by, but it wouldn't be too bright. She left the office heat on and closed the door.

Then she went to work mopping up water. She'd come in early today. Wanting to make sure things got tidied before people came to decorate.

Clare unlocked Skye's door. Skye had asked her to clean up on the days she wasn't coming in and Clare wasn't sure if she was back yet. Her room looked the same as usual, except for the pools of water on the floor. So she mopped in there as well, leaving the stones where the being had left them.

Then closed the door and locked it again.

Clare switched on the fairy lights in the back corner. The ritual space looked absolutely enchanted. She could almost forget the being had come again last night. Almost.

By the time she'd gotten everything cleaned up and a pot of tea made, Jenny arrived.

"Good morning," Jenny said.

"Hello. There's a surprise in the office," said Clare.

"What?"

"Well, it wouldn't be a surprise if I told you, would it?"

Jenny went to the office and peeked in the door.

"Oh my goodness," Jenny whispered. "They are adorable. Everything went all right then?"

"I didn't see any problems," said Clare. "Pirate hasn't gotten up this morning. But she looks okay. Just tired."

"So cute."

Jenny closed the door. She hung her purse and coat on the rack.

"Let's not tell anyone yet besides Marcella, and Skye if she comes in, okay?" asked Clare.

"Okay. You're right. Pirate needs some peace and quiet. But I can hardly wait till the kittens have their eyes open and are running around."

Clare nodded.

Marcella came flying in the front door.

"Sorry I'm late," she said, breathlessly. She ran to the back and hung up her belongings, then went into the front straightening her orange peasant top and smoothing her hair down.

Jenny laughed and poured herself a cup of tea. She turned on the sound system for the shop and went out front to began straightening things out.

Clare sipped tea and bagged up the packing debris from yesterday. Then she broke down the boxes and stacked them on an empty shelf for recycling.

After the first rush of customers, she quickly vacuumed the back room. Then roped off the aisles between the shelving, filled with back stock. Then she was done with the back room at least.

Just after one Kristin and Raven came, their arms full of boxes with branches of dried and fresh foliage sticking out.

Clare led them to the back.

"Oh wow," said Kristin. "This looks so cool. I really didn't get why you wanted all the fabric, but it makes sense now. This is gorgeous."

Raven said, "Amazing. I saw it last week when I came for a massage, but you hadn't moved the shelves yet. What a transformation."

"I'll turn on the overhead lights so you can see to work."

Clare slipped into the office. Marcella was standing just inside the door, looking at the kittens.

"They are so cute," she said. "And Pirate's such a good mom."

"They are, aren't they?" said Clare.

Some of them were awake and nursing. Others asleep.

It looked like Pirate had eaten some of her food. She was bathing one of the kittens, purring away and ignoring the spectators.

Clare sat down at the desk and took care of email and some billing.

Marcella said, "Well, I'm off to run some errands and go home to change for tonight. What are you wearing?"

Clare looked down at her black boots, black trousers and green blouse and said, "This. I won't have time to go home and change. I was just going to go grab dinner somewhere."

There was a knock at the door and Kristin stuck her head in, "Hi, I was wondering if Skye was coming in today?"

"I haven't heard from her," said Clare.

Marcella said, "Kristin, Clare's planning on wearing this tonight. Don't you think she should wear something more festive?"

Kristin stared at Clare's clothes.

Clare suddenly felt like a teenage girl again. Wearing clothes that just didn't measure up. And neither did she.

"I've got an idea," Kristin said. "I'll get you something. Emma's looking for ways to boost her business and you need to kick off your event series in a big way. I think you'll both benefit."

She popped back out and closed the door.

"See?" said Marcella. "Well, I'll be back about six. I think people will come early tonight."

"Great," said Clare. "I might still be getting dinner. We'll see. I'll leave the heat on. Just turn the store lights off while no one's here so it looks like we're closed."

Marcella left.

Clare tried to concentrate on finishing things up, but was too distracted by Pirate and her kittens.

Occasionally, one of them would mew and Pirate would pull it closer to her belly, towards a nipple. If Clare listened close enough she could hear the kittens purring.

Their ears were folded close to their heads and eyes still closed. They were so tiny she could have fit a kitten in the palm of one of her small hands. They couldn't really move on their own yet. Pirate pulled them around.

The little white one had been rolled on its back and had the same black heart shape under her chin that Pirate did. The tip of its tail was black as was a spot on one tiny paw.

The gray tabby had extra toes on its front feet. The black kitten looked like it was totally black with no white. The gray also looked like it had no white. She couldn't see the orange one. It was on the bottom of the sleeping pile. Only its brownish nose stuck out.

The tortoiseshell kitten had a half black, half orange face with the line going perfectly down the middle of her pink and black nose. All the kittens were very fluffy, just like Pirate.

Clare stared at them for a long time before she realized she'd lost most of an hour. She felt a little hyper. Excited about the events of the day. She'd better check and see how things were going out front.

She saved the computer file and closed it.

Then slipped out of the room.

Jenny was helping two customers and it looked like she didn't need any help. Clare went into the back. Raven was working on setting up an altar in the center of the mats.

She'd spread a rust colored cloth and was putting black candles and stones on it. They looked like obsidian. There was an almost knee high, slate gray stone statue of a Sheela na Gig, a goddess sculpture found on many ancient churches. The stone carvers who built churches hadn't necessarily been Christians.

Raven looked up and said, "What do you think?"

"I like it." She noticed there were four other altars. One for each of the four directions. They'd used the corner table for one and brought in three other small tables. Each was covered with a cloth and dried branches with leaves or rose hips or other cut branches. There were tall pillar candles, stones, feathers, sculptures.

"You two have a lot of stuff."

"That's what happens when you get old. You collect more stuff every year. I just don't have a good stone for the water altar. One that carries the same weight as the others." She gestured to the altars.

Clare spotted a large piece of carnelian on the fire table, a hunk of green Connemara marble for earth and an ostentatious piece of lapis for the air element.

"I think I've got just the stone for you," said Clare.

She went to one of the long aisles and unwrapped one of the stones they'd gotten in the shipment yesterday.

She carried the chunk of boulder opal back to Raven, who was now standing. The rock was only partially polished, leaving other parts of it rough. The opal had leaked into the cracks of the host stone and looked like rivers running through the sandy colored stone. It had a stunning play of color and light, in blacks, blues and greens. The stone was the size of one of the kittens, filling her palm.

"This is from Australia. I don't know what the base stone is."

"Oh my gosh. That's perfect. How much is it?"

"You don't have to pay to use it tonight," said Clare, surprised.

"No, I mean I've got to have it," said Raven. "It's extraordinary."

"It is, isn't it? I love this company. They send me the coolest stones. Let me look and see how much I paid for it. I ordered so much from them this time that I can't remember prices off the top of my head."

"Let me know please. I really, really want it," said Raven, rolling it around in her hands. "I've never seen one like it."

"I got two, but the other has a lot of red in it. Wouldn't work quite so well for water."

"I like this one."

Raven set the stone down on the water table. It set off the altar nicely.

"Where's Kristin?"

"Something about clothes, I think. She'd forgotten to bring what she's wearing tonight?" Raven shrugged.

Clare glanced at her watch.

"I'm going to close up the store soon and run to get tea. Are you going to stay here? I'll need to lock the door to keep customers out, but I don't want to lock you or Kristin out."

"One of us will stay. The other will go eat. I know Mary's coming early with some snacks for tonight. It's okay if we eat back here, right?"

"No problem. After the ritual, we'll sweep off the mats and roll them up till next time. I'll vacuum the whole place tomorrow. And I'm locking the office. Pirate's in there."

"Pirate?"

"Our shop cat."

"You can let her out. She won't bother me," said Raven.

Clare hesitated and then said, "She just had kittens last night. The Vet said not to disturb her for a week, so she can bond with them. No playing with kittens for seven days," she said, in the Vet's deep voice, waggling her finger as Jenny had done in imitation.

Raven laughed.

"Can I peek?"

"Peeking is allowed. But don't spread the word. I don't want to let everyone who comes tonight peek."

She opened the door slightly and they peered in. The kittens had been rearranged again. Different ones were nursing and others sleeping. Pirate didn't even look up at the two intruders. She continued sleeping. Clare could hear her loud purr over the kittens purrs and mewls.

How was it possible to purr and sleep at the same time?

She and Raven pulled their heads out of the doorway, Clare pressed in the back of the knob, locking it and then closed the door.

"Oh my gosh," said Raven. "They are too cute. If they don't already have homes, I'd love another cat. Lucy needs a friend. We lost Abigail last winter and she's been awfully lonely."

"I don't have takers yet, but my staff hasn't really gotten a chance to see them. I'll let you know though."

Raven put her hand over her heart and said, "This is really auspicious timing. Here we are in the depths of darkness, Samhain. We're concentrating on what we want to seed into our lives. What we want to give birth to and here's these new lives beginning. Wow."

Clare smiled.

Jenny had just locked the front door and said, "You don't want me to close out the cash register do you?"

"No. But we should do a quick vacuum in front. I did the back this morning."

"You go get tea. I'll vacuum, then go get mine."

"Deal," said Clare. She got her coat and purse, looked around and checked her mental list. Office locked. Store locked. Everything else taken care of.

She went out of the shop, walked down the street into the cold wind and tried to decide where she should go for tea.

And where was Skye? It was unlike her not to check in. Clare had texted earlier in the afternoon, but she hadn't answered.

She hoped everything was okay.

Most of all, she hoped the being wouldn't show up again tonight. That it would go away and never return.

Chapter 12 ~ Skye

Skye woke with a start. It was completely dark outside and the room felt far too hot. She sat up, still feeling groggy. Taking her mobile from the nightstand, she saw it was six. And it was dark outside, so evening.

The radiator clanked on. She couldn't turn the heat off, the house manager controlled it. So Skye cracked the window open a bit, letting in the cold air.

It took her some time to realize she'd been out for nearly twenty-four hours. Dreaming and having the worst nightmares. Her human body was well rested, but her sylph body felt awful.

Afraid and nearly frantic. From nightmares of tortured sylphs.

Her mobile had a text from Clare and one from Marcella.

Marcella's said "Kittens!" and had a photo of Pirate with six adorable kittens.

Clare's said, "Haven't heard from you. Hope everything's well. Getting ready for the ritual tonight. Hope to see you."

Crap.

She'd forgotten. It was Samhain.

Skye stumbled out of bed, trying to wake up. She went into her bathroom and splashed cold water on her human body's face, cupping her hands and sipping from them. The cold water tasted refreshing, but didn't seem to be enough to wake her up.

Her human body smelled sweaty and didn't feel very clean either.

She ran through a quick, cool shower, trying to keep her long braid mostly dry. Why had she made a human body with long hair anyway?

She dressed all in black. Boots, black jeans and a turtleneck. Then unbraided the braid and pulled her hair loose a bit. A whole day in the braid made it kinkier and more untamable than ever. She pulled her fingers through some of the worst tangles, feeling the knots unravel with using just a hint of magic.

She glanced in the mirror.

All the black looked a little stark. She put a tan vest on to break things up a bit. Grabbed the light blue coat, stuck the mobile in her purse as she shouldered her small bag and left.

She ran down the street towards the main part of town. Partly to wake herself up and get the blood flowing, partly to escape the cold, cold wind.

Her stomach growled. She hadn't fed this body for a long time. Days.

Skye slowed to a walk and pulled her mobile out. It was nearly seven.

She stopped by the grocer's shop and bought an apple and some cheddar cheese. Then ate them while walking to the store. The apple was crisp and sweet. It went really well with the heavy, sharp cheddar.

By the time she got to the shop, Skye felt okay. Physically at least. She was still disturbed by the nightmares and her trip to Faerie.

Nothing to be done though. She sure hoped Meredith and Dylan were coming tonight.

The store was lit up and she could see people inside. Clare was at the cash register, talking to someone Skye didn't recognize.

Marcella was at the door and unlocked it when she saw Skye.

"Hey, I got your text."

"Good. We hadn't heard from you and were worried."

"I didn't sleep much on my trip, did it all when I got home."

Marcella nodded.

Skye waved at Clare and went towards the back. She heard mewing coming from the office and smiled. Kittens.

She went to her room and unlocked the door. Then slipped out of her coat and hung it on the hook along with her purse. She checked her mobile to make sure the sound was still off and put it in the purse. Then picked up the stones the being, the Fomorian, always used and set them on one of the shelves outside her room. Skye pushed her massage table back to the center of the room and tidied everything up.

She stood in her room, taking a few minutes to breathe and center herself for whatever might happen tonight.

Then went out, locked her door and slid the keys into a pocket. She walked around the corner of the shelving to see the ritual space. It looked glorious.

A few people were already seated around the circle. Jenny was adjusting a branch of dried leaves in a vase.

Skye went back out to the front of the store, noticing someone had hung hooks on the ends of the shelves for people's coats plus more hooks on the wall. That Clare. She thought of everything.

Clare was still at the cash register, but the people who came for the ritual were all milling around.

"Hi," said Skye. "Sorry I didn't get in touch earlier. I didn't really sleep on my trip and I got back late last night. I just got up an hour ago. And ran here."

"Wow. That must have been some trip," said Clare.

"It was and not necessarily in a good way. But things will either work out or not. I'll just have to wait and see."

"I'm sorry. We were just worried about you."

"I'm fine," she lied. "And Pirate had kittens!"

"How did you know?"

"Marcella texted me a picture."

"They're so cute."

"Is there anything I can do to help?"

"I think everything's under control at the moment."

"Are you okay?"

"I'm nervous. But I'll be okay. Growing pains, you know?"

Skye nodded.

"Well then, I'll just wander around. We start at 7:45?"

"That's what the flyer said. I think we might give it a few extra minutes. Emma's not here yet. And we're fairly short for the number of people who said they were coming. But it's early yet, it's not even 7:30."

Skye nodded and wandered through the store. There were items put out that she didn't recognize. More new books. New jewelry must have come in. More fairy houses of course.

The fairy houses always made her smile. Bumblebee houses maybe. She didn't know any Fae that tiny.

The people who were in the shop, mostly women, but a couple of men, were all dressed up. Some fashionably, others in costume. The predominant costume was, of course, a witch.

Not very original, but very common. When Pagans celebrated All Hallow's Eve or Halloween, as they called in it the U.S., they mostly dressed as witches.

There were a couple of fairies, complete with gauzy wings and shimmery short skirts. And an ogre. One of the men was dressed as an elf, with his long blond hair nearly covering the pointy ears.

Marcella opened the door for three other people and in walked a short, lumpy older woman, carrying the end of a mermaid's tail. A slender young man dressed as a merman followed her.

Another man followed. He was tall and muscular, wearing what looked like a cyclist's outfit, tight leggings in red, orange and yellow. He had on snug red gloves and a mask, or was it face paint that covered his bald head with scales of crimson and burnt orange? He wore contacts to make his eyes appear to have no whites, just a yellow iris with a dark, slitted pupil.

He took her breath away.

The heat coming off him felt so welcoming, like wading into a hot spring.

She stood staring at him for what must have been five minutes.

The mermaid and merman walked up to Skye and stood in front of her.

Skye peeled her gaze away from the orange man to look at the people in front of her.

"Skye?" said the merman, laughing.

She recognized Dylan's voice. It was only then that Skye felt the immense amount of power they carried.

"Oh hell," she said, embracing him. "I didn't recognize you in the costume. Not even the eyes."

He laughed, "That was the idea."

She hugged Meredith.

"I can't tell you how happy I am to see you."

"Tell me that again at the end of the night," said Meredith.

She turned to the orange man.

"I'm Aidan," he said.

"Skye." She held out her hand to shake his, pretending he was human. Even through his glove the heat rippled off him, shot up her arm and through her entire body. It felt disconcerting and wonderful all at the same time. "Amazing costume."

"Not all of it's costume," he said. "I didn't have time, well, you know."

She nodded. He'd come on short notice. No time to make a human body.

"You have a nice costume too," said Dylan, staring at her clothes.

"It's sort of an ironic one that I just threw together. Human. You know."

Aidan laughed.

It took Dylan a minute before he got the joke. Then he joined in the laughter.

"We should go into the back," said Skye. "But I want you to meet Clare. She owns the shop."

She took them around the counter towards the back and introduced them.

Clare smiled and was polite, but she looked hesitant.

"These are some of the friends I went over to Ireland to see."

"Oh, well welcome," Clare said.

Skye said to Clare, "If anyone can help us with our night visitor, my friends are the ones."

"Really?" said Clare, looking hopeful.

"We'll see. Afterwards."

Clare nodded.

Skye followed the others to the back. They stood near the back of the circle, as close to the front exit as they could. People were gathering in the back, but it seemed like it would be a while before things got started.

Skye asked, "How did you get here?"

"We took a ferry, then a train. It seemed the best way," said Dylan.

"And people didn't stare?" asked Skye.

"Only Meredith and I spoke. With American accents. We told them we were celebrating Halloween. Everyone seemed to buy it. Those who didn't were too polite to say anything."

They were standing in the area just outside Skye's room.

Meredith said, "I can feel the problem. Well, we'll be here if something happens. If not then, like you said. Afterwards."

"You heard that?" asked Skye.

"My ears aren't blunted by a human body."

"Yeah, my senses are so dull. I'm really worried. Can I tell you what happened on my way back here?"

"Certainly," said Meredith.

They huddled together and Skye told them.

When she'd finished, worry hung heavy on Meredith's face.

"After tonight is over, we'll need to talk. There are strange goings on. That's one of the reasons we brought Aidan."

He nodded, but said nothing.

Skye felt more afraid than she had last night. Sylphs weren't known for their courage, but for their speed at flying from danger.

But after last night, it felt like even flying was dangerous.

Chapter 13 ❦ Clare

Clare stood in the front of the shop. Moving books so they aligned, tidying up the rack of new pendants. Most of the celebrants were in back. Waiting to begin. The electricity in the air was palpable.

Marcella was at the door, ready to lock up. Everyone was there except Emma.

Raven had just texted her and Emma said she was on her way.

Clare rearranged a group of candleholders again. She took a deep breath, trying to calm herself and counting to seven as she exhaled. She repeated it six times and felt a bit clearer, but not more calm.

Clare had almost given up waiting when Emma rushed in through the front door.

"Sorry I'm so late. I'm not usually like this. But Kristin told me you needed something for tonight and I almost had this finished. It's just perfect for your coloring," she said, breathlessly.

She held out a long sleeved, silky beaded top of paisley in brown, black, tan and rust.

Clare gasped, it was stunning.

"This is gorgeous, but I couldn't possibly…"

"Yes, you can. You need to wear something powerful as you step into this new life you're beginning. Now go put it on."

Clare took the top and walked towards the back. Emma followed her. Marcella stayed by the front door, ready to lock up in a few minutes.

Clare was going to use the loo, but the door was closed and the occupied sign was clicked on.

She unlocked the office, slipped the keys in her pocket and went inside, closing the door behind her. Pirate looked up, rolled over slightly and went back to sleep.

Clare slipped out of her shirt and put the paisley top on. Then turned to look in the mirror hung on the back of the door.

It was gorgeous. Emma was right. It made her feel beautiful and even powerful. The beads shimmered slightly in the light. The fabric felt warm and comforting. The cut of the blouse even made her look slightly curvy. Which she wasn't.

Clare left the room.

Emma was standing outside, having taken her coat off and hung it up.

"Perfect," said Clare. "It's beautiful."

"It's just right for you."

"How much do I owe you?"

"It's gratis. Just tell people where you got it from when they ask," said Emma.

"I couldn't…"

"Yes, you could. Clare, you need to learn to accept gifts."

Her mouth snapped shut. Emma was right. No one had given her gifts as a child and as an adult she still had a hard time accepting them.

"Thank you," she said.

"You are so welcome," said Emma, grabbing her hands and enfolding them tightly. Then she let go and smiled.

Raven walked up and said, "Well, do you think we're ready to begin?"

Clare glanced at her watch. It was 7:45.

"I could start my spiel," she said. "That'll give us five more minutes."

"Good. Are we missing anyone that you know of?"

Clare shook her head. "I think everyone's here, plus a few." There were more than thirty people in there. Probably closer to forty.

"Well then, let's begin," said Raven.

Emma and Raven went to join the circle. Clare followed. A woman stood holding a woven basket out. It was filled with mobiles.

Emma put hers in the basket.

"Please make sure it's off," said the woman to Emma.

Emma took her mobile back, shut it down and set it back in the basket, grinning sheepishly.

"Mine's off and in my purse," said Clare. Earlier she'd turned off the sound for the shop phone as well.

Another woman stood with a bowl of water and sprinkled it over the top of their heads. The water was from the White Spring, one of two sacred springs in town, and the sprinkling was a purification. A passage into ritual space. Clare remained standing at the edge of the circle closest to the door.

As Emma and Raven sat down, everyone became quiet. The room was dimly lit by the fairy lights on the walls and backs of the bookcases. There was a feeling of expectation floating in the air that Clare could almost touch with her fingers.

"Good evening and blessed Samhain," said Clare. "I'd like to welcome all of you here tonight. I'm Clare Grigson and

I own this shop, Sacred Space. Tonight begins a new cycle for all of us, including the shop. Beginning tonight we'll be offering seasonal rituals like this, as well as other events: lectures, readings and workshops. The schedule is beginning to take shape. There are flyers by the cash register that are a skeleton of what we'll have. You can sign up for our mailing list out front or online. The schedule is up on our website and I'll do my best to keep it current. Feel free to ring us if you have any questions. I'd like to introduce the life and blood of the shop. You already met Marcella at the front door. She knows an amazing amount about everything. Jenny, who keeps us all focused, is over there."

Jenny waved.

"Skye is our resident, and amazing, massage therapist. Her business cards are at the front desk."

Skye rose up onto her knees and waved.

"And Pirate, our shop cat, is extra busy tonight. You'll have to meet her during her normal working hours. That's our staff. We'll be open for a while after we finish here, so you don't need to rush off. For those of you who don't know her, I'd like to introduce Raven who will be leading us tonight. She's an extraordinary tarot reader. If you're looking for an understanding of what's going on in your life, ring her up. Her business cards are up front as well. Raven?"

Clare stepped back into the shadows towards the front door. She waved at Marcella who locked the front door and then switched off the lights in front. They had agreed Marcella would wait out in front for another few minutes, since this was the first event here at the shop. It wouldn't do to have people banging on the door to get in.

Clare went to the edge of the circle and sat down, listening to Raven.

Raven stood next to the center altar, dressed completely in black. Her blouse and skirt covered with a long velvet cape. It was open enough to see strands of silver necklaces beneath. Long black and silver hair just added to her imposing figure.

"Blessed Samhain everyone. This is yet another incarnation of rituals that I've led for years. Tonight we celebrate the turn of the seasons from the harvest to the darkness of winter. It is in that darkness that our new seeds will sprout. During the ritual I'll use the term Goddess, for the Earth is our Mother. You may choose to replace that word with one that suits you better. Everyone is welcome here."

She continued, "We'll invite the directions and our guides to join us. Then, once the circle is closed, we'll ask you to stay inside this sacred space. If you must leave, please do so quietly. We'll come to the bulk of our work tonight. Afterwards we'll release the directions and break for snacks and conversation."

Raven walked around the circle looking at people as she spoke.

"Emma, would you call the directions?"

Emma stood, shaking a rattle made of tinkling bells. She began to walk around the outer edge of the circle and said, "Spirits of the east. Spirits of air and wind. The winged ones, the flying creatures. New beginnings and open horizons. We welcome you and ask you to join us, gifting us with your wisdom and blessing."

Miranda was standing over at the altar for air, on the east side of the room. She lit the candles and moved away from the altar.

Emma said, "Spirits of the south. The fire of the summer sun. The snakes and salamanders, the heat lovers. Igniting our passion, creativity and love. We welcome you and ask you to join us, gifting us with your wisdom and blessing."

Miranda lit the candles for the fire element on the south side of the building.

Emma continued, "Spirits of the west. The water surrounding us and the season of fall. The swimming beings, whales, seals, the finned ones. Surrender and trust. We welcome you and ask you to join us, gifting us with your wisdom and blessing."

Miranda lit the candles for water on the west side of the building.

"Spirits of the north. The tall mountains and the deep caverns. The bears, deer and other animals. The solitude, peace and darkness of winter. We welcome you and ask you to join us, gifting us with your wisdom and blessing."

Miranda lit the candles for earth on the north side of the room.

Emma said, "Spirits of the center. The mystery within, eternal, ageless and unknowable. Our guides and ancestors. We welcome you and ask you to join us, gifting us with your wisdom and blessing."

Raven lit the candles on the center altar.

"The circle is cast," she said and set the matches down. She stood up again.

Clare could smell the sulphur from all the matches mingled with the melting candle wax.

"Samhain marks the first day of winter for us in the Celtic world. For many it's a time of connecting with our ancestors. Of giving thanks for the blessings they've passed on. Of acknowledging their presence in our lives still. But tonight, I think we should choose to look forward. The Earth is in a world of hurt. The polar icecaps are melting. Animal habitat is shrinking. The water itself, our lifeblood, is being poisoned. Giant corporations control too much of the world, wreaking destruction on our children and grandchildren's heritage and those companies are untouchable. Our politicians, bought by big money, stand around bickering about inconsequential things while our future is at stake. Our world stands on the brink of devastation it can't recover from. For humanity the past is filled with darkness. The evil we've done to each other. Our future is uncertain. What we do in our daily lives will perhaps affect it. Perhaps not. One thing is certain. It's only right now where we have the power to act. We can't be in the past or the future. We've only got now. I'd like each of us to consider what we can do as individuals, and as a collective, to change things. Tonight is for our world. Our original ancestor."

A woman Clare didn't know picked up a bhodrain, an Irish round drum, and began tapping on it gently with a beater. The drum's deep voice sounded out.

The woman began singing in a lovely, clear voice, "Isis, Astarte, Diana, Hecate, Demeter, Kali, Inanna." She repeated the refrain and others joined in. By the third time everyone was singing and standing.

It was an old chant. Clare had no idea who created it or when. As everyone chanted, she felt the energy in the room rise. It felt alive and almost tangible. She felt connected to the group as together they wove the sound. The rhythm of the music swirled around her, voices rising and falling with the tune.

Clare found herself lost in the music. She swayed with the rhythm. Went deep inside herself and stayed with the group all at the same time. When the woman stopped drumming, maybe about fifteen minutes later, everyone stopped singing at the same time. As if they'd all agreed to the timing in advance.

"That's what I'm talking about," said Raven.

A few people laughed.

Clare hadn't felt that connection for a very long time. Since before she left Manchester. She'd gone to a couple of rituals with a friend. That had been her inspiration for opening the shop. A search for community.

She took a deep breath and let herself feel the contentment. Deeply.

As Raven moved around the circle, she spoke about her everyday life.

"I take electricity, water, gasoline, food, fabric, plastic, paper, wood furniture, a house made of bricks and who knows what else. Glass, too. We depend on Gaia for our sustenance, our creativity, our nurturing. And we take, take, take, but rarely give back. Organic farmers at least give back as much as they take. They water and nourish the soil. Make compost to feed the soil. The rest of us, not so much. I'd like you to get comfortable and close your eyes."

Raven paused, sitting down.

"Imagine yourself walking down a road. A gravel road. It turns into a dirt trail. Surrounding you on all sides is an abundant hedgerow, filled with hazelnuts and rose hips, rowan berries and apples. There's a gap in the hedgerow and you cross through. Into a grassy meadow. There's a large flat rock in the center and you go sit on it. The sun beams down, and although it's the end of fall, you're warmed by its presence. Now, I want you to take in the scents of the sun on your skin, the ripe apples and the damp earth. There are birds in the hedgerow, working the berries. You can hear them talking to each other. A breeze blows through and caresses your skin."

She continued, "I want you to feel this vibrant Earth that surrounds you. Feel it all the way down to your bones. You come from this Earth, you will return to it when you die. You are made of stardust and spider legs and all the people ever born. If you are taking part in destroying the Earth, and aren't we all, then how are you not destroying yourself at the same time? The violence we do to the Earth is violence we also direct towards ourselves. I'd like you to sit for a few minutes and think of the ways you personally are responsible for disrespecting our planet. This isn't a guilt trip, we just need to pry loose some of our thinking around habits that we take for granted. What are you taking too much of from the Earth?"

Clare made a quick mental list: she received too much packaging that wasn't recyclable for store orders, she used a lot of electricity to run the store and probably kept it too warm, she took a lot of long hot baths, she didn't buy much organic food because she was always going out to eat, her mobile and computers weren't exactly made with environmentally safe products. The list went on and on.

After a time Raven said, "I'm going to pass around paper and pens. I'd like everyone to take one and write down one thing you're willing to change in your daily actions towards Gaia."

Clare was the last person to get the pen and small pad of paper. She wrote down, *Contact vendors and ask them to change their packaging. Explain why it's important. Give them an ultimatum?*

Raven lit a charcoal tablet in the iron cauldron sitting on the center altar.

"I'd like you to all come and put your paper into the cauldron. Let's burn the past and take one step towards living more consciously on this green Earth."

Clare stood and followed the others over to the cauldron. She dropped her paper in and watched it burn, then went back to her space to make room for the next person.

There wasn't much smoke from the burning paper, but Clare was glad she'd taken the smoke detectors in this room down and put them in the office, until after the ritual.

When everyone had finished Raven nodded to the woman with the drum. She began another chant.

"She changes everything she touches. Everything she touches changes."

They started out singing together, then someone took it an octave higher. It was beautiful. Clare hadn't sang for a very long time. It loosened up the tight, rigid places in her soul.

She needed to sing more often. She needed more music in the store. Perhaps the drummer would be willing to lead a workshop. Ideas spun through the air and Clare had more possibilities spring into her mind than she could do in a lifetime.

As soon as the ritual was over, she'd need to write them down.

The drumming and singing stopped.

Raven said, "Sustainable changes begin one person at a time, one tiny baby step at a time. That's how we'll get there."

Raven sat down and everyone else followed.

She said, "Does anyone want to share what they want to change? I'll pass this hazel stick around and while you're holding it no one else will speak. If you don't want to speak, pass it on to the next person."

Raven passed it to the young woman on her left, who took the stick and spoke up.

"I drive too much. I've been meaning to talk to my company about telecommuting, but just haven't gotten up the nerve. It would save so much petrol, wear and tear on my car, plugging up traffic. It's time."

The woman next to her said, "I'm the manager of a small office. I've been meaning to set up a better recycling system. And haven't. I'm also the first one in and the last one to leave. So many times I forget to turn lights and heat off. It's just wasted energy. I need to focus on that more. And don't get me started about the styrofoam cups in the lunchroom. I just need to replace them with paper and tell everyone to go to hell!"

Laughter broke out.

The next person, a man said, "I'm guilty of everything. Heat on too much, driving too much. Leaving the telly on all night. It's time to clean up my life."

People continued to go around the room, some talking, some passing the stick on. All of Skye's friends passed, as did Skye. When it was Clare's turn, she took the stick, noticing the intricate carvings on it.

She talked about her thoughts on packaging and the need to stand up and make a statement to her vendors.

Then passed the stick on. When they were finished, Raven set the stick on the altar.

Raven said, "Marion's going to drum for us for a while. I'd like you to close your eyes and return to that stone in the meadow."

The drumming began, setting a slow rhythm and Clare closed her eyes.

"I'd like you to feel the warm sun on your skin. Hear the birds singing and flitting around in the hedgerow. Watch the long meadow grass wave in the breeze. Clouds blowing across the sky. Sit down on the rock and feel its solidness beneath you. Now, from the far end of the meadow you see a shadow approaching you. It could be a spirit, or a person. An animal or the Goddess herself. Each of us will have a different experience. This being has a message for you. I want you to listen to it and remember it."

The drumming continued.

Clare felt herself in the meadow. A bee buzzed on a yellow flower close to her. Clare kept looking down the meadow. She couldn't see anything. No shadow. No one was coming.

Then the bee landed on her arm.

Oh.

She asked, 'What do you have to tell me?'

The bee thought at her, "*Be strong. Be solid. Be yourself. It's you that's needed here. Your strength and quick thinking.*"

Then it buzzed off and disappeared.

She sat.

What was that about?

She wasn't strong. Or solid. Or quick thinking.

Raven said, "When you've gotten your message, or had an encounter, return to this room. Come into your body. Stretch gently and open your eyes."

Clare opened her eyes and sat, still thinking about what the bee said.

When everyone was back, Raven picked up a silver bowl filled with stones.

"I collect rocks, as some of you may know. Wherever I go, I pick them up. I buy them when one calls out to me. I can't bear for stones to go unappreciated. Periodically, I have to go through the house and set some of the stones free. Some end up in my back garden. Others, well I'm passing this bowl around so you can see if any of these stones speak to you. See if one augments the message you received in the meadow. Don't give it a lot of thought, just feel."

When the bowl made it around to Clare, she was drawn to a stone that was silver with yellow crystals spread throughout it. Roundish and about half the size of her palm, it was partly smooth as if slightly polished by machine. It felt cold at first, but warmed to her touch. It reminded her of the bee.

She smiled and rolled it back and forth between her palms. It was heavy. The silver must be some type of metal. The weight of it in her hand reminded her of the baseball she used to throw at the house as a kid when she was angry with her parents.

Raven said, "Spirits of the center, the mystery with everything. We thank you for your presence here tonight. Go if you must, stay if you will. We release you." Then she blew out the center candles.

Emma stood by the north altar and said, "Spirits of the north, the peaceful dark winter. We thank you for your presence here tonight. Go if you must, stay if you will. We release you."

Miranda snuffed out the candle with her fingers.

Emma had moved to the west altar. "Spirits of the west, the colorful autumn. We thank you for your presence here tonight. Go if you must, stay if you will. We release you."

Then she moved to the next altar as Miranda pinched out the flame.

"Spirits of the south, the heat of summer. We thank you for your presence here tonight. Go if you must, stay if you will. We release you."

Emma moved to the final altar, Miranda snuffed out the flame on the south altar.

"Spirits of the east, joyous spring. We thank you for your presence here tonight. Go if you must, stay if you will. We release you."

Miranda pinched out the final candle.

Raven rose and said, "The circle is open, but unbroken. May the peace of the Goddess stay in our hearts. Merry meet, merry part and merry meet again."

She continued, "We have treats cooked by Mary and things to drink. Please hang around and socialize. I'd like to point out that Clare isn't charging us for using this space, so if you'd like to leave some money either in the basket on the treat table or buy something in the store, we'd all appreciate it. She and her staff have gone to a huge amount of work and expense to create this gorgeous space. Let's repay them."

Everyone else got up.

"And don't forget to get your mobiles back from me on your way out," said the woman who'd collected them all in a basket.

Clare moved towards the front of the store and switched the lights on. Marcella unlocked the front door. Clare checked to make sure everyone's business cards were stocked up and that there were enough schedule flyers near the cash register.

Raven came out of the back next. "Oh my, I don't think I've ever experienced a ritual so powerful! I was having a hard time channeling all that energy."

"I think it went wonderfully," said Clare.

"Well good. I'm going to step out front and cool off," she said, leaving the store.

Marcella said to Clare, "That top is so gorgeous. Is it new?"

"Emma."

"Wow, I've got to get over to her shop one of these days. That is just perfect on you."

Jenny came out front munching on a piece of gingerbread and holding a cup of tea.

"You have got to have some of this gingerbread. The lemon sauce is divine."

"Oh, I'll go get some," said Clare.

"No time like the present. You go back and schmooze. We'll hold down the front," said Jenny.

"Okay." She went into the back. The blouse really did make her feel wonderful. She loved the way the fabric slid over her body, so soft and silky.

She chatted people up and answered lots of questions about the schedule. It seemed everyone had a friend or a friend of a friend who gave classes and wanted a new venue. Clare figured she could have every single evening booked at the store for the next year if she followed all the leads.

She'd have to make a plan. Tomorrow.

Tonight was for celebrating.

Clare got lots of compliments on her blouse and she pointed them all to Emma. Finally, she told Emma, "You need to give me some business cards for your shop."

"I'll need to get some printed up. I just haven't had the time. Too busy designing and sewing."

Kristin came over and joined them.

"This was such a fabulous ritual. I think everything turned out well."

Emma nodded.

Clare said, "I do too."

"People are so happy to have found a place to celebrate," said Kristin.

Clare dished up some gingerbread and lemon sauce. It tasted divine. The ginger, cinnamon and cloves in the cake were perfectly balanced and the lemon of the sauce complemented it.

Mary was a short, plump woman. She stood by the food table and served tea and hot cider to those who wanted it. She'd brought the hot beverages in two massive thermoses.

"This is delicious," said Clare.

"Thank you," said Mary. "I blog about cooking all the time. I'm going to put the recipe up on my website if you want it."

"Alas," said Clare. "I don't cook."

"Never?" said Mary.

Clare shook her head. "I just don't make the time. And even if I did learn, I just can't squeeze in the energy."

Mary said, "It's hard, I know. I work at home, so I'm always cooking. But then I love it."

Faerie Contact

Eventually, the crowds thinned until only Skye and her three quiet friends, Raven, Miranda, Emma, Mary, Jenny and Marcella were left.

Raven, Miranda and Emma were disassembling the altars, putting things back into the cardboard boxes they'd brought them in. Mary was ferrying the food out to her car. Jenny was cleaning up and Marcella was closing out the cash register.

Clare helped Mary take a last load out and Mary drove off.

Clare went into the back. Skye was showing her friends the massage room. Clare went into the far back and helped Raven stow her things into boxes.

Raven said, "Thanks for selling me this gorgeous opal, Clare. I just love it. I have the perfect place for it."

"I'm pleased it found an appreciative home," said Clare. "I love rocks too. I've always collected them." She pulled the silver and yellow stone from her pocket.

"What is this, do you know?"

"Oh, that one's so cool. It's a pallasite meteorite. The yellowish stone is olivine and the silver is metal of some kind. Found in the States, the midwest somewhere. It's lovely."

Be strong, be solid, be quick thinking. What had the bee meant?

Clare heard a strange schlopping noise around the corner of the shelves. She stood and walked out to look.

Just this side of the hallway stood a huge dark shape. It was taller than most people and wider. It looked vaguely human shaped, but it's facial features wouldn't stay in one place. Neither would its limbs. They seemed to come and go. The form was a blue so deep it was black and it dripped water. It smelled of salt, kelp and seawater.

The creature looked like dark water held in by a membrane. That changed shape.

It filled her with terror. She could feel herself beginning to shake.

"Skye," said Clare, as calmly as she could manage. Even her voice shook.

Skye immediately appeared by her side, as did Skye's friends.

The orange man in the biking costume moved towards it, as did the older woman. The mermaid. Clare couldn't remember any of their names.

She backed farther into the ritual space. What should she do? Her eyes searched for a weapon, anything. She pulled aside some fabric and opened the cleaning cabinet. Grabbed the mop.

Skye had disappeared. Raven, Jenny and Miranda stood in the far back, looking terrified.

The mermaid and orange man spoke in a language Clare had never heard before. The being growled at them in what sounded like the same language.

It lashed out at them. Swatting the woman towards the shelving with a watery arm.

The man shot a flame at the creature.

The being recoiled then hit him. The orange man went down. A cloud of steam filled the area.

The merman ran towards the thing, but couldn't even get close.

The thing shot a burst of water at him. Pushing the merman against the wall of shelves outside of Skye's room. It pinned him there.

The old woman was up and backing away from the creature . She was doing something with her hands. Clare couldn't tell what.

A tall blue woman with iridescent wings came out from Skye's room. Clare had never seen her before. She looked fierce. She blew strong winds at the creature who hissed at her like a snake. Stalking towards the creature, she blew it against the far wall from where stood.

The creature roared at her. The merman was standing again. He and the mermaid streamed jets of water at the being. They backed it against the wall. The orange man threw a blast of flame at it. With the blue woman's wind, the flames grew huge, catching on some of the fabric on the wall. Steam and smoke rose, blowing through the entire back room.

The being shrieked, in rage or pain, Clare couldn't tell. It broke free from the water, wind and fire it was blasted with and began to run towards the hallway to the front.

Just then the office door opened and Marcella stood in the doorway.

"Marcella! Get back! Quick," yelled Clare.

Marcella did, but too late.

The creature stopped. A black and white blur flew out of the room and down the hallway at the being.

Clare sucked in her breath. She didn't know what to do, couldn't get close enough to hit it with the mop, not with the flames. Not that a mop would do much damage.

She pulled the stone from her pocket.

Be strong, be solid, be quick thinking.

Pirate stood hissing at the creature. Ears pinned back she yowled and attacked it, claws out, leaping at its middle.

The being shrieked. Water poured out of it. Pirate leapt back as it swatted towards her. Then she was back in again, raking its legs. The two spun in a half circle, Pirate in for an attack and out again. Probably fighting for her life and her kittens.

Clare held the stone in her right hand and summoned up every bit of energy she could. Aimed and threw the meteorite like a fastball aimed at the bully who'd lived down the street and picked on her sisters when they were all kids.

She had poured every drop of anger, of hatred and pain that she'd ever felt in her life into that throw. Every feeling of violation from her childhood till now.

The stone hit the being in the middle of the face.

The creature yelped and ran towards the large puddle on the wood floor, away from the wind, fire and water. The being dropped completely out of sight, water splashing everywhere.

Pirate shook herself like a dog. She was soaking wet. Then stalked towards the office door, sat down outside it and meowed plaintively.

Clare could hardly breathe, let alone speak.

The old woman passed by the large pool of water and opened the office door to let Pirate back in.

"You can come out now dear," the old woman said, to Marcella.

Marcella ran out of the room towards the back, warily avoiding the puddle.

The old woman closed the door to the office.

"What *was* that?" asked Marcella.

"I think that was our night visitor," said Clare, looking at the mermaid, merman, orange man and the blue woman.

The blue woman nodded. Her face looked paler before and her pale blue eyes were wide. Clare noticed she had knee length, braided white hair.

Raven said, "What is a night visitor?"

Clare turned to her, leaning on the mop that she still held.

Raven, Miranda, Jenny and Emma stood huddled together.

Clare sighed. She spotted her stone in the middle of a trail of water. Picked it up and dried it off.

She had no idea how to explain things. She didn't even know what the creature was.

Clare stood staring at the pool of water on the floor. Was the creature just lying in wait beneath the building? Had it sunk back into the Earth? Would it return?

She shivered.

Chapter 14 ❦ Skye

Skye closed her eyes and concentrated on the Earth beneath the building. She could feel the Fomorian retreating. Down a tunnel. Then he hit the water table and followed a trickle that became larger and larger. He swam with great speed moving towards the sea.

Skye opened her eyes. Dylan was doing the same thing. Except he still followed the Fomorian. He was more skilled at water magic.

Clare asked, "What exactly was that?"

Skye said, "He is what you would know as a mythical being. A Fomorian. One of the old gods. From before the Tuatha de Dannan even."

"What was it, he, doing here?" asked Clare. Clare kept looking at her strangely and Skye realized Clare didn't recognize her.

"Searching for answers," said Meredith. "I believe it's time to come clean."

Skye sighed with relief.

Meredith continued, "We are Fae. Dylan here, Aidan and Skye. Myself included."

Skye watched as Meredith gestured to her, when saying her name. The humans all looked shocked. None of them had ever seen her before, not in Fae form.

"So you are Tuatha de Dannan?" asked Miranda, her eyes widening.

"Our ancestors were," said Meredith. "Recently, the Fomorians have begun taking those of us living out in the world, prisoner. Many of us have died torturous deaths. Skye, Dylan and I were among those who escaped. We returned to Faerie to warn them. Then the Fomorians attacked Faerie, bringing the boundaries down. We imprisoned the Fomorians, or so we thought. We should have realized that they too had children over the ages. That was one of them."

"Will it come back?" asked Marcella.

Dylan's eyes were open now.

He said, "I don't know. He has returned to the depths of the sea, for now."

"So did he come here for you, Skye?" asked Raven.

"I don't think so. He first came the night before I'd even come to the shop. He might have kept returning because of me, though."

Skye watched Clare's face droop even more. Skye felt fear and hopelessness wash off her friend. She looked at the other humans. They all needed some reassurance.

Skye said, "Let's go sit in the back and talk."

"I should clean up the water," said Clare. She was looking at the scorched wall, covered with the remains of burned fabric and melted fairy lights.

Skye put a hand on her shoulder and said, "Later. You've had a long day. The water's not going anywhere. Tomorrow I'll help you clean up the mess on the wall."

"I'll take care of it," said Jenny. She took the mop from Clare. Marcella turned off the lights in front and made sure the door was locked.

Everyone else went and sat back in the circle, to the left side of the center altar, which hadn't been taken down yet. The room felt strangely empty, now that the crowd of people was gone. Raven held up the matches and looked at Skye.

Skye nodded.

Raven lit the candles and the glow helped hearten Skye. The fairy lights were off, or had shorted out, so the ceiling lights were still on. The room smelled of smoke and sea. They sat in silence for a couple of minutes.

Dylan was pulling his merman's tail off to reveal a pair of jeans. His chest was still bare. Aidan removed his gloves. Skye noticed the backs of his hands were scaled. Just like Egan's.

"Don't look at me," said Meredith. "I'm not taking off anything. I don't think you humans want to see that much nudity right now."

Skye laughed. Meredith was trying to put everyone at ease.

Miranda said, "None of us had any idea what you really looked like, Skye. That you were Fae. How did you manage to look human?"

Clare nodded.

Skye said, "The human body that I created, I normally wear like clothing almost. When I remove it, it would look like a dead, empty body to you. A suit of skin. But it's not really alive, so it can't be dead. It's like a very ornate and complicated set of clothes.

"I didn't think it was possible for you to be any more beautiful," said Jenny, who'd finished mopping up and joined them. "I'm pleased to see what you really look like."

"Thank you," said Skye.

Raven said, "I thought the ritual felt incredibly powerful, but the energy felt almost peculiar, alien. Not like anything I've ever felt before, now I know why."

"So, now what?" asked Miranda. "Why are you all here?"

"Have any of you humans ever seen anything like the Fomorian?" asked Meredith.

"No," said Raven.

Everyone else was shaking their heads.

"Well, that's good," Meredith said.

"What does it mean when you said the boundaries are down. For Faerie?" asked Raven.

Meredith gave a deep sigh.

"Faerie is a complicated place. There are many of us and we are so different. Skye is a sylph, Dylan is a water sprite, Aidan is a creature of fire. I am of the deep sea. There are dryads and undines and spirits of the stones. None of us is the same. Which means we often want different things. Very long ago, when humans were beginning to spread themselves over the earth, to trespass on our world with their technology, our ancestors decided to close Faerie. To make it unfindable by humans. So they changed Faerie so that it existed in the same area as humans. It overlays your world, but is closed to you. It's a very complex spell. By doing this they also enclosed the energy of Faerie. It didn't flow any more and it didn't renew itself. Faerie became stagnant to those who lived in it. Our elders began to wane and die. Waning was almost unheard of in Faerie, not any more. Some of us didn't agree with the closing and we chose to leave Faerie. To make our lives in what was becoming the human world. So when the Fomorians tore our boundaries apart, we were vulnerable. With no boundaries, it means we must make peace with humans."

"So that's why you're here?" Emma asked Skye.

"Yeah. Some of us who've lived among humans for thousands of years are better equipped to be…ambassadors," said Skye.

"Skye, and others, are out in your world, in places where people might be receptive to meeting us," said Meredith. "We're trying to let people know we exist."

Faerie Contact

"Without scaring them. Some of us aren't exactly the beautiful, winged sylphs that Skye is," said Aidan smiling.

"It's true, some of us are lumpy, watery creatures," said Meredith, laughing.

Skye looked around. Everyone was watching Meredith, completely spellbound by her story, human and Fae alike. She was a natural leader, just like her brother Varion. She should have been Luminary, not him. But she'd already left Faerie by the time he was chosen.

"The Fomorians have often been at war with us. It seems their children will be as well."

"What happened to them?" asked Miranda.

Meredith gave another great sigh.

"The Fomorians attacked Faerie. They unraveled the boundaries, bringing down the barriers and began exterminating Fae as they moved towards the center of Faerie. We imprisoned them. We thought we got all of them. But it seems others have been wakened and are looking for their leaders."

"What will you do now?" asked Clare.

"I don't know. We must return to Faerie and tell the Luminary, Egan. Then we must decide."

Marcella said, "So, tell me if I'm right. Faerie is like another country, which is situated where? And the Fomorians are an army, most of whom you're holding prisoner. The others are looking for them. This all sounds political. Shouldn't you contact the surrounding governments and let them know what's happening?"

Skye said, "It *is* political, but human governments won't be able to handle the Fomorians. When the boundaries were taken down Faerie happened to be in the West of Ireland, but it has the ability to move. See, the thing is, magic really exists. Even stagnant, Faerie is filled with it. The Fomorians have powers that can destroy the entire world if they were given free reign. They don't have the same ethical viewpoint you humans do. They're gods and they can do what they want.

Take what they want, destroy whole cities with the flick of a finger. They've been sleeping for centuries, while you've built your entire civilization. Then they woke up. Lucky for you they were focused on destroying Faerie, so they pretty much ignored you."

Jenny said, "My head hurts just thinking about it. I hate violence and politics."

Meredith said, "This is Faerie's problem to solve and I should tell you that Faerie is no longer stagnant. The elders are waking up, renewed. Those that are still alive, at least. But no matter what happens, everything has changed."

"In what way?" asked Clare.

"For Faerie to wake up means that magic is loose in the world again. Humans with magic capabilities will begin to realize it and use their power," said Meredith.

"And not all of them have the wisdom to hold such power," said Skye.

"So, how can we protect ourselves from that?" asked Raven.

"If you're a human with any ability, you should hone it and use it to become more aware of what's happening around you," said Skye. "I have to admit, Sylphs aren't into bravado. We don't go hunting down the bad guys. We tend to get out of the way and let those more qualified do it."

"And who's qualified?" asked Miranda.

Skye said, "I don't know," she gestured at the other Fae.

Meredith said, "We're going to have to answer that question, us Fae. I don't have an answer right now. You have to understand that the Fomorians we have imprisoned control winds, and drought. The sea. I'm not talking about some of the latter Greek or Roman deities. They controlled love, hearth and home, crops. The Fomorians are similar to the Titans, the Greeks primeval gods. The Fomorians controlled nature to such a degree and were so powerful, so elemental, that none of us knew how to stop them. That's why we imprisoned them."

"I still think you should talk to governments," said Marcella.

"I agree they should be warned," said Aidan. "But how? They have no experience with magic. They don't even believe it exists. What do you think they'd say if I walked into one of their offices and told them that story?"

"They'd call you a nutter," said Jenny. "No doubt about that."

Clare said, "So your plan was to infiltrate the human world, spread the word of your existence, begin to show yourselves and then approach humans as a whole? Approach governments?"

"Yeah, something like that," said Skye.

"We were hoping we had more time," said Meredith. "Time for humans to get used to the idea that they share the planet with beings who are more powerful."

"Time so humans wouldn't panic," said Raven.

Clare said, "Well, I feel panicked. There's a being, a god you're telling me, who's been coming into my shop every night for months. Tonight he came during an event and we all got to meet him. He attacked, perhaps in self-defense. I'm afraid for my friends, and myself. I can't even think about putting people at risk again, like this."

Skye could see tears pooling in the corner of Clare's eyes. She could feel a heaviness settling into Clare's chest as her words hit home.

"Clare," said Skye, putting her hand on Clare's arm. "Now is not the time to be making any decisions. Wait and see. It's possible he won't return. He might go elsewhere. Take the path of least resistance."

Clare took a deep breath and nodded.

Skye didn't feel sure of anything. Not about the Fomorians or about the missing sylphs. They had to be connected.

The only thing she knew was that things would get much worse before they got better.

If they did get better. Meredith, Dylan and Aidan all looked grim. Meredith said nothing more.

Chapter 15 ~ Clare

Clare's alarm was chiming. Over and over again. She managed to put her feet on the cold floor and stumble across the room to it.

The awful sound stopped. She was almost back into the comfy warm bed, beneath the comforter, when she asked herself, what day is it?

Monday. It was Monday.

She plonked down on the bed. Sitting, her feet tucked beneath her, legs crossed. In the cold air.

She pushed away remnants of the awful dreams from the night before. It was about the being. The Fomorian.

She shivered.

Time to wake up and get ready to open the store.

Why had she thought it would be a good idea to be the person opening the night after an event?

To give her staff time off.

Clare rubbed her face, trying to wake up. Her mouth tasted awful. She hadn't brushed her teeth last night and after all that sugary food, it was like something had died in there.

She uncrossed her legs, putting her feet back on the cold floor. Opened the closet door and put a robe on. Slid her feet into soft slippers.

She went out into the kitchen and poured water in the kettle and got it started heating.

Pulling out the large metal travel cup and lid, Clare grabbed a tin of strongly scented black tea. She was going to need a lot of it to get going this morning.

An hour later Clare left her house, zipping her coat up against the frozen air while juggling the mug of tea.

She opened the sipping slit on the lid and drank the strong hot liquid while walking. The cream tempered the strength of the black tea, adding richness.

The day was dark with clouds. Samhain had come and gone. Winter was taking hold now.

The sidewalks were pasted with wet leaves. The trees had almost finished dropping them, but a few hardy leaves clung to the branches.

Clare walked quickly, trying to wake up, warm up and get to the bank and the shop on time.

At the Sacred Space, she unlocked the door, went in and locked it again behind her.

She went to the back hallway to take off her coat.

Pirate meowed at her.

Clare opened the door.

Pirate was lying in her box, nursing kittens, but her food bowl was empty and it was clear she'd used the litter box.

"Good morning dear, I'll get you some food in a minute."

The smells from the office made her realize that there was no Nag Champa scent lingering in the building.

The Fomorian hadn't come back last night after being chased off. Didn't mean he was gone for good, though she hoped he was.

She put her hand in her jumper pocket, feeling the heavy meteorite.

Walking towards the back, she felt relieved everything was just as she'd left it last night. No pools of water.

A day's reprieve on mopping up salt water.

She stared at the wall where burnt fabric still hung. That was where Aidan had blasted the being with flames. Dylan had put it out with a stream of water. Clare pulled the ladder out and climbed it to examine the wall. The flames had mostly gotten the fabric. The wall bore a black spot, but it hadn't gone deeply into the surface. A spot of paint should cover it. Then get some more fabric and rehang it. Well two of the colors were coming down anyway. Only the scarlet would stay for next month.

She turned the heat up in the store. Got some Alasdair Frasier fiddle music going on the music system and loaded up the cash register.

Clare fed Pirate, refreshed her water, emptied the litter box and refilled it.

She squatted next to the box, petting Pirate as she ate. The cat had the loudest purr.

The mewling kittens were so adorable. She'd have no problems finding homes for them, even though part of her wanted to keep them all.

Well, maybe just one.

She glanced at her watch. Time to open.

"I'm going to leave your door open for a bit. Let some fresh air in."

She turned the heat up in the office so the kittens wouldn't get cold.

After unlocking the front door, she checked messages. One from Raven, telling her she'd done a reading and not to worry. The being wouldn't return to the store.

Another from Emma, saying that the ritual last night was absolutely lovely. The best one she'd ever been to and thanks for letting them use the space.

Clare still felt dubious about whether the being would return or not. If it did, there could be no more evening events. She picked up the schedule and put them in the office, to wait a week before deciding.

Tourist season was definitely over and the morning was slow. Clare used it to tidy up the front of the shop. Whenever a large group of people came through, like last night, things got put on shelves where they didn't belong.

After she'd organized everything, Clare went to the back. The mats were still down. She swept them off and rolled them up, putting them up on a shelf with the yet unused, colored mats. Then she closed the office door so the cats wouldn't be disturbed and vacuumed the back.

She'd leave the fabric up until it was time for the next season. Sometime in December. Then she'd take down the brown and rust fabric. The green and white fabric would come out to accent the scarlet.

There was a large delivery and she spent some time putting away the books, more jewelry and an order of ritual supplies. Her order of new tarot decks came in as well.

She had only a couple of customers. Which was a relief. Clare liked having the occasional day when she could simply get things done.

She sat at the desk in the office and went over the sales from last night. Made lists of things to reorder. It had been a very good night. If she continued to host events and the sales were always this good, then she could hire another part-time person to help out. That's what she'd been counting on. Neither Marcella or Jenny wanted to work several nights a week. They didn't need any extra hours.

She hadn't heard from Skye, who'd wisely not scheduled any massages for today.

Part of her felt betrayed by Skye's deception. But really, who would have wanted a massage from a six foot tall winged sylph? Even with the almost hypnotic magnetism she exuded. Clare probably wouldn't have even rented her the room if Skye had first appeared in her real form.

Who was Skye anyway? How much of their interactions had been a deception? Clare really needed to know the answers. She needed to talk to Skye.

She felt conflicted. but she wouldn't do anything to discourage Skye from continuing to do massages. She really helped people.

Clare just didn't know what Skye hoped to accomplish working here. It wasn't like she was going to walk around the store in her sylph form. Or out on the streets.

How was giving massages while masquerading as a human helping to expose the world to Faerie and the fact that Fae were now roaming the Earth? And perhaps always had been. Maybe even before humans showed up.

Clare had no answers and that really bothered her.

She'd been absolutely stunned last night, when Skye and her friends revealed themselves. And shocked when she saw the Fomorian. It was one thing to clean up after it every morning, quite another to see it in reality.

Her entire world had flipped over. She had to figure out this new reality.

What exactly had happened when she threw the meteorite at the Fomorian with all her pain and anger?

She shuddered and ate a bite of her tuna sandwich, toasted at home in the morning and warmed up in the microwave. The food tasted good. Her stomach wasn't feeling great after so much tea.

The food helped ground her. Helped her deal with all the strangeness of the previous night.

She'd meant to ask Skye if she knew what lay beneath the building. How was the creature getting in? The largest pool of water was in the same place every morning. Right where Clare had seen him last night.

If it hadn't been in the middle of the hallway, she would have found something big and heavy to put there. But he seemed to be almost made of water. So fluid he created new limbs when needed. So he might just have oozed around anything she put on the floor.

Just like he oozed through the floorboards when he disappeared.

She shuddered again.

"Stop. Just stop torturing yourself. Think about something else," she said, aloud.

Clare finished her sandwich and went over to pet Pirate, who was nursing two kittens. The others were sleeping.

"What shall we name your kittens, my dear? I know when they're old enough to go to their new home, their people will want to name them, but they're going to be hanging around here for a while. We'll have to call them something."

She picked up the all black one. It mewed slightly and then began purring as she stroked it.

Pirate watched her.

"I'm not going to take your babies. I just want to meet them."

She put the black one down next to Pirate and picked up the orange one, stroking it for a minute, before putting it back. She did the same with the gray tabby and the tortoiseshell. The white and the gray one were nursing, so she let them be.

She went back to the desk and cleared away her lunch debris. Then closed the office door and went back out into the store.

By the time she'd shelved all the tarot cards and books, in the back and a few out front, it was time to close up for the day.

Clare fed Pirate again, tidied up and closed everything down.

Then walked home through the cold and wet to leftover soup.

All her questions left unanswered.

Her entire future felt like it was hanging in the air. Waiting, at the whim of other beings who she didn't understand.

She'd never been good at waiting.

Chapter 16 ~ Skye

Skye had felt helpless sitting in the back of the bookstore with Meredith, Dylan, Aidan, Clare and the other humans. Smoke from all the candles hovered in the air. The altar in the center was the only one still intact, the others taken down. Everyone had sat talking, in a circle on the mats, to one side of the altar.

All of them talking about what should be done now. She wasn't participating.

Skye just sat there, arms wrapped around her long legs, her wings gently fluttering. Afraid. She felt trapped by the knowledge that Fomorians were loose in the world again.

All Skye could think about was that she really hadn't had enough power to halt the Fomorian.

Why did they terrify her so?

Was it because they had held her prisoner for so long? Painfully long in that cold iron cell. Just thinking about it gave her the shakes. She tried to push the dark horror away.

Meredith and Dylan had been prisoners as well, but they hadn't been afraid to face the Fomorian. Although they said the cold iron hadn't affected them as much as it did her.

Was it because all the other air elementals had gone missing? Her friends and family vanished.

Or could it be that she was just such a coward?

Her long hair, wet from sweating inside the human body draped over her skin, making her feel cold. She was rarely cold when in her own body. But she felt paralyzed. Frozen.

Meredith wanted to take the information back to the other elders in Faerie, before coming to any conclusions. What she wasn't saying could fill volumes.

Skye slipped back into her human body, silently apologizing to her wings, once again, at having to fold them up and smother them.

The Fae left the store and the humans, who seemed out of harm's way for the present. The humans were packing up and getting ready to leave as well.

As they walked towards Skye's flat, they made decisions. Meredith was going to return alone to Faerie. She felt safe enough to swim alone. She'd send others back to protect Skye, Adaire and the other Fae out in the human world. Dylan was going to follow the Fomorian. Aidan was going to stay with Skye who seemed in the most danger.

"What will you say to them?" asked Skye.

Meredith replied, "I don't know. We still haven't come up with a plan to defeat the original Fomorians. We know the vault can't hold them forever. But now, if there are offspring, and they're awakening I don't know what we should do. It may be that we'll need to close Faerie again. And be fighting those outside the barrier and trying desperately to find a solution to keeping the others confined to the vault."

"So war inside and out," said Aidan.

"Yes. I can think of no other solution at the moment. And I hate that one. I'm hoping the other elders can come up with something better. I do know that the Fomorian from last night was strong, I don't see how we could fight several offspring as well as the ones in the vault. Their power is so different than ours. I don't know how to shut it down."

Skye felt deflated by Meredith's reaction. She'd hoped the elder had a plan, because if she didn't, then it was unlikely that anyone would come up with something.

They said their goodbyes and Meredith raced into the night, moving incredibly fast, having shed her costume. Dylan went off in another direction, presumably following the Fomorian.

Skye and Aidan walked down the street.

"I don't know how I'll get you up into my flat," she said. "I'll probably need to get another place to live. One that can take two people."

"Do you have a window?" he asked.

"Yes, and there's a tree outside it."

"I'll climb then," he said. "Then, I'll make a human body now that I have time and I know I'm staying."

"I'll talk to the landlady tomorrow. See if I can pay extra rent."

The night was cool, but dry. The wind was up and the air smelled fresh and crisp. It blew her hair around.

She couldn't feel excess heat coming off Aidan's skin the way she had with Egan.

"Why aren't you exuding heat like Egan does?"

"Egan runs a lot more heat than I do," said Aidan. "I'm more skilled at controlling it. He told me he used to be able to, when he was living in the human world. But ever since the accident, it's something he struggles with."

"You're just the right temperature," said Skye. He made her feel warm and safe.

It had been a long time since she'd felt completely safe. Since long before she left Faerie, over two thousand years ago.

At the house, she showed him the window. Then she went in through the front door. There were people in the common room, watching a horror movie on TV. Having a party.

"C'mon on in and join us."

"No thanks," she said. "I'm tired, going to bed."

Inside her room on the top floor, she locked her door and opened the window. Aidan was already up the tree and waiting. He jumped to the window sill and crawled inside, surprising her with his agility.

She closed the window and switched the electric heater on to supplement the radiator.

"Well, what now?" she asked.

"Are you tired?"

"My human body is. It needs to rest." She took off her coat and boots, then got into bed.

Skye slipped out of her human body and covered it with the blankets.

She got her mobile out of the purse and put it on the charging base, turning on some soft music to mask their conversation. Then they went and sat on the floor between the radiator and the electric heater.

She unfolded her wings. They always got slightly damp from being folded inside the human body and she fluttered them, drying them.

Aidan said, "Now, do you know what the dark cloud that followed you back from Faerie was?"

"I can only assume it was a Fomorian. I have no ideas other than that. At the time I believed all the Fomorians were locked in the vault beneath Faerie, although I suspected the being in Clare's store was one. It just felt similar."

"Felt…"

"I don't know how else to put it. I sensed something that was like the other Fomorians. Not that I got that close to them."

He nodded.

"Can you tell where he is now?"

She closed her eyes and took her consciousness to Clare's store, leaving behind her body. The store was empty, except for Pirate and her kittens. Skye slid beneath the floor boards and into the tunnel beneath the store.

She went down the damp tunnel. She scented the water and followed the Fomorian to underground river and slid into the cold rushing water. Following the current as it became progressively saltier and she was in the sea.

Skye followed the Fomorian's trail into the depths. Then she caught another scent of energy.

Dylan.

He was ahead of her, following the creature.

He must have sensed her and waved her off. She returned to her body in the room, sitting by the radiator with Aidan.

She shivered from the cold and felt him touch her arm. Heat spread throughout her as Aidan increased the amount he radiated.

"The Fomorian's still deep in the sea. Dylan's near him. I followed the Fomorian once before, to the same place. Did he make the trip back to Clare's store every night? What was he looking for?"

"You?"

"I don't think so. The first night he came before I'd even rented the back room."

"Clare's store has a magnetic effect. You know that, right? Meredith, Dylan and I sensed it before we even got there."

"Ley lines, perhaps. That's what the humans call them, lines of energy and power. They run all through Glastonbury. I wonder, is that why I chose to go in and ask about renting the space, even though I had no indication there was a room in the back?"

"Perhaps," he said. "I think the draw is also from Clare. She's closed. But it's as if she's got a large amount of tied up energy that she doesn't know what to do with. She's extraordinarily powerful, but doesn't have an outlet, a channel."

"I noticed that when I worked on her. Yet, when she spoke tonight, the room was riveted. She glowed with power and people were held by her words, as if she bestowed a sense of harmony on them. She's a leader. So you think the Fomorian was attracted to that? Even though he came at night, when she's not there. Why didn't he go to her house."

"I don't know. She leaves her energy around the store. It's everywhere. I watched her. She spends a lot of time organizing and touching things. Perhaps the path to the store was more direct."

"Then, she's the one in danger, not me."

"Who can say?"

"What exactly made the Fomorian leave, Pirate attacking him or the meteorite she hit him with? Or us Fae?"

"I don't know. Perhaps all of it combined. I don't understand why the three of us Fae attacking him had so little effect. Are the Fomorians really that powerful? I wasn't nearby when the other Fomorians were imprisoned in the vault."

"My head hurts just thinking about them," said Skye.

"You need to rest."

"I've been resting, sleeping in the human body. For almost twenty-four hours."

"Sleeping in a human body when your mind is troubled isn't resting."

"You're right."

"May I?" he asked, holding his hands towards her head.

"You're a healer?" she asked. Why hadn't she been able to sense that in him? It was unusual for a fire spirit.

He nodded.

"Okay."

She moved closer and he put his hands on her head. She felt the gentle heat move through his fingers and into her skull. It felt as if he was massaging her brain.

The heat increased and she felt herself growing drowsy. She curled up on his lap and his hands stayed on her head as she drifted off into worlds of diaphanous clouds and peach-colored sunrises. Floating on thermals.

Chapter 17 ~ Clare

The next day went much the same.

Except that she'd slept horribly all night long and woke with aching muscles on the left side of her back. She felt sluggish, made cold cereal for breakfast. She ate without tasting anything. Then dressed in a navy turtleneck and trousers. Clare struggled to put on blue socks and slipped into a pair of clogs so she wouldn't have to bend over again for the shoes.

She stumbled off to the bank and the shop. Every time she moved wrong, which was often, shooting pains spread through her body from the left side of her spine.

Thankfully, there were no pools of water. The being hadn't come back last night either. Clare felt a small measure of relief, but she still wasn't ready to believe the Fomorian was gone for good.

Not long after she'd opened, Marcella got there and began tidying up the packing materials and boxes.

Clare lit two lemongrass candles, hoping the gentle aroma would clear her head. She walked around the store, sipping Earl Grey tea with cream. Tidying already perfect displays. She couldn't sit for long, it hurt too much. Couldn't stay in any one position for long. It felt better to keep moving.

An hour later Skye came in, looking bright and cheery, dressed in a cherry red T-shirt, sky blue leggings and a cream colored light coat.

"Good morning," she said.

"Good morning, how are you?" asked Marcella.

"Morning," said Clare.

She was still unable to reconcile this waifish blonde haired woman with the bluish tinged skin, huge iridescent winged powerful Fae she'd seen the other night.

"I'm doing wonderfully," said Skye.

Clare noticed she was beaming. Almost glowing with light.

She caught a glimpse of a handsome man with long, dark hair out on the sidewalk. He waved at Claire and then disappeared down the street.

"Who was that?" asked Clare.

Skye turned towards the window and said, "Oh, that was Aidan."

"Aidan?"

"Tall, orange, red, and yellow, scaly guy from the other night. He's a fire spirit," said Skye. "He's staying with me."

"And that's his human body?" asked Marcella. "He's so hot. But he's yours, isn't he?" she said, to Skye.

"I'm not sure yet. Perhaps. It's hard to tell with Fae. But he's definitely here to protect me."

"But he's not coming in?" asked Clare.

"I don't need protection here. Especially, while I'm in this human body."

"But what if the Fomorian returns?" asked Clare.

"I don't think the Fomorian was here for me," said Skye.

"Then who was it here for, or what?" asked Marcella.

"I'm not clear. But it wasn't me. I sort of think he was looking for a safe, secure place to be. On land. He always went to my room, yes, but all he did was sit in the circle of stones. It was as if he was seeking a vision of some sort. Looking for something. Possibly the other Fomorians."

"Do you think he'll come back?" asked Clare.

"I don't know. Has he returned since we confronted him?"

Clare shook her head.

"Then hopefully, he's decided this isn't a safe place anymore or maybe he found what he was looking for. I sure hope it wasn't more Fomorians.

Clare felt her muscles contract with fear.

A customer came in the door and Marcella went to help him.

"Are you okay?" asked Skye, "You just turned white as a sheet."

"Fine. I'm fine."

Clare reached over to pick up her cup of tea and winced from the pain.

"You've hurt yourself," said Skye.

"I slept wrong," she said, moving towards the office.

Skye followed her into the back.

"Listen, I don't have an appointment for a couple of hours. Why don't you let me work on you? If it's still okay, now that you know what I am." Skye stood looking at her, head cocked.

"Does it matter what I think?"

"Of course it does. I'm sorry I couldn't tell you before. I thought about it, wanted to. But what could I have said? *'Hi, I'm a six and a half foot tall winged Fae, a sylph. And I'm a healer.'* You would have either laughed at the silliness or run in the other direction."

"You're right. I wouldn't have believed you existed. My mother used to talk about Fae all the time. *'The Faeries will punish you if you don't behave,'* that sort of thing. I never believed her. So, I'm still trying to shake out the Fae don't exist bollocks. It's not leaving without a fight."

"Let me go set up my room, turn the heat on. You can finish up your opening stuff and then I'll work on your back. It looks painful."

"Okay," said Clare. "I don't think I have much left to do."

Skye nodded and went in the back towards her room.

Clare put in another order for stones and crystals. They'd sold a lot of them the other night.

Then rinsed out her teacup and put it on the desk. Pirate and the kittens were all sleeping.

She closed the office door and told Marcella she was going to get a massage.

"Nice," said Marcella. "I'll take care of things."

Clare knocked on Skye's door.

Skye opened the door and went back to adjusting the music. Clare walked into the room, sat on the chair and slipped off her clogs and stepped on the toes of her socks to pull them off.

Skye left the room, closing the door. Clare finished undressing, hanging her clothes on the hook. She gingerly lay face down on the warm massage table. Putting her face down through the hole in the table and pulling the sheet over herself.

The heat felt lovely and her body nearly melted into the table.

Skye knocked on the door.

"Come in," said Clare.

"How's the music?" asked Skye.

"Haven't even noticed it. I'm still asleep this morning."

"Are you the right temperature?"

"I feel all lovely and melty."

"Good."

Clare could hear the squelchy sound of Skye rubbing oil on her hands.

"So," said Skye, pulling the soft sheet down to Clare's waist. "Your back hurts the most here?" Skye laid a hand on the exact spot, between her shoulder blade and spine.

"That's it."

"And you said you got it from sleeping on your side wrong? Not from straining it?"

"Yep. Was fine last night. This morning after sleeping badly, it hurt like hell," said Clare.

She could feel Skye spreading oil over her entire back. Her hands strong and warm.

"What kept you from sleeping well?" asked Skye.

"Worrying about the Fomorian."

"Like I said, I'm thinking he's gone."

"But you're not sure," said Clare.

"No. I won't lie to you. Anything else?"

"I'm worried that he'll come back. I'd like to move forward with scheduling the events for the store, but I can't do that until I'm sure he's gone."

"Life is full of insecurities. You could never be sure that an earthquake or fire wouldn't happen and people would be trapped, perhaps even die in the building."

"True, but if I knew there was a dangerous being coming to visit often at night and I hold evening events at that time, then…"

"Okay. I get that. But so far, he's gone. Give it a few more days, but keep planning, just keep the schedule to yourself. Tell people you're still nailing things down. But I think for your sanity, you need to assume things are going to be just fine. You've got a huge amount of energy that's stuck. You can't do that. It forms knots in your body like this one."

Clare could feel as Skye gently touched the sore spot.

"That's from being in turmoil?"

"Yep. You're holding on to a lot of tension. Stuff you need to let go of because you can't control any of it."

"But how can anything be safe if there's a war going on between Faerie and the Fomorians? A war with the elements?"

"They're not exactly the elements, they simply control aspects of those elements. There's nothing you can do about it. That's the business of Faerie. Of those in Faerie who understand politics. I don't. I don't claim to have any solutions to the problem. Which is why I'm here, in the human world. Where I can help, at least I think I can. It's out of your control."

Skye's fingers kneaded the muscles surrounding the knot in her back. Almost as if untangling yarn, gently pulling the strands apart so they wouldn't knot more. Every now and then, she'd move her hands around to work on Clare's entire back, giving the knot a break. Then she'd return and work on it some more.

"You know, you did a great job the other night. Organizing everything and making things run smoothly. Your introduction was awesome and set just the perfect tone."

"Thank you. I put a lot of thought into everything."

"It showed. You were wonderful. You should do more events here. That's why I'm pushing you to keep going. I've been to a lot of rituals, human rituals. You have a gift. It's not for any of us to squander out gifts."

"I just don't like being responsible for other people. I guess I thought I was done with that."

"You've done it before?"

"My entire childhood and well past my teens."

"Who were you responsible for?" asked Skye.

"My parents were semi-functioning alcoholics. They grew worse as they got older. I started working, while going to school, as early as I could. Bringing in some money so my younger sisters wouldn't have to be ashamed of having shabby clothes. I kept working after I finished school, sometimes two jobs. I gave most of the money to my sisters to buy food, I'd moved out and was living with roommates. When my sisters got older and married, I stopped taking care of anyone else. I cut everyone off financially and they all quit speaking to me. Guess they only saw me as free money. That didn't mean I began taking care of myself. I worked just as hard, two jobs. Saved the money until I could afford to open the shop."

"Wow. So in all that taking care of your sisters and your parents, was there any time for you? For having fun? Was anyone taking care of you?"

Clare felt a deep pool of sadness spread throughout her entire body. Her eyes began to leak, salt water pooling around the edges of the face hole of the massage table and dripping on the floor below.

"No. There was no fun. No time for me, just for the future. There was no one to take care of me, but me. Since I quit working two jobs, I've been slowly trying to learn how. I'm not there yet."

"You've got time. One thing to learn, that many humans need to learn, is not to be so hard on yourself. We're all works in progress. Even us Fae, although some Fae would be too arrogant to admit such a thing."

"I'm working on it," said Clare.

"You clearly have to add in some time for fun."

"I don't even know what fun is."

"What an adventure you've got ahead of you then. How many days off a week do you give yourself?" asked Skye.

Her hands returned to the knot again. She pressed on it for a few minutes and told Clare to breathe.

Clare could feel the emotional hurt deepen as Skye put pressure on it. She took a deep breath, then exhaled. Skye let up on the pressure.

"There, the knot's released a bit. I'm going to work on your hands and arms."

She covered Clare's back with the sheet and got more oil.

"So, how many days off?"

"One, maybe none. Depends on everyone's schedules."

"You need to hire another person."

"If the events succeed I can add another full-time person or even two part-time people."

"Well, then we need to make them succeed. You need at least two days off a week. And perhaps you should do some experimenting with things that sound fun. Go hiking. Or skydiving. Or learn how to play chess. Whatever sparks your interest."

"Once I can manage more time off, I'll look into it."

"Promise?"

"Promise."

"Well okay, then. I think you're going to be just fine."

Skye continued the massage and Clare slipped off into visions of having time to just walk around the village or walk the long path up the Tor.

Had she kept herself too busy the last few years, just so she wouldn't have time to feel all the pain and hurt any more? She'd gone through therapy. More than once, trying to deal with her childhood or lack of one, and her parents' neglect. The hurt lessened, but never went away.

Now, she was in charge of her life. And had about as much control over it as any adult.

It was time to let the pain go.

She needed to learn, and fast, how to nurture herself. To Mother herself. To admit that other than the Goddess, there was no one else who could do it, or would do it.

It was time to take charge of her own life.

Chapter 18 ❧ Skye

Skye moved around her room, cleaning up. Her last client had just left. She turned off the heater.

The room felt closed up, too warm and claustrophobic from a full day of body work.

She needed to get outside for a walk. Feel the cold wind blowing on her face. Even if it wasn't exactly *her* face.

Skye switched off the heater. Then stripped the massage table moving to the beat of tabla drums. Putting the used cream-colored sheet in the woven basket, she closed the top. They'd need to go to the laundromat tomorrow. Then she shook out a clean pale green sheet and floated it onto the massage table. Smoothing out the wrinkles and tucking the ends neatly beneath the pad so the sheet wouldn't slip when her next client got on the table. The she got another sheet out and draped it neatly over the top.

She turned the drum music off, slipped her mobile out of the player and into her purse. Glancing around the room, she made sure everything was set up for her next session, which would be tomorrow.

Then she slipped her black wool coat on over the rose colored tunic and black leggings. She put her purse over one shoulder and left the room, closing and locking the door behind her.

Skye went into the front of the store, luxuriating in the cooler air. The grounding smell of sage came to her nose. Jenny must have been burning it. She was dusting a glass display shelf of athames, when the front door burst open.

In rushed a harried-looking Adaire. Her long hair had been blown about by the wind, her gestures looked frantic and distressed as she tried to restrain the long black hair and dripping green raincoat. She wore a large khaki backpack over her shoulder.

She looked out the door behind her, as if expecting to be followed.

"Good afternoon," said Jenny.

"Uh, hi," said Adaire.

Skye went up to her and asked, "What's wrong?"

Adaire hugged her and whispered, "I need to talk."

"Sure, come back to my room."

She led Adaire into the back, unlocked her room, turned the light on and closed the door after them.

Adaire just stood there, looking numb.

"Sit down. Can I get you some tea?"

Adaire nodded, "Tea would be good."

The dryad took off her backpack and plopped it heavily on the floor. Then sat on the straight chair.

"Black?"

Adaire nodded again.

Skye hung her purse back on the hook and slipped her coat off, hanging it over the purse. Then went out to the hallway and poured a mug of tea from the teapot Jenny had started earlier.

Jenny said, "Do you know her?"

Clare was in the office and looked up from the computer.

Skye said, "She's an old, old friend."

"Fae?"

"Fae. A dryad."

Jenny nodded, a smile of satisfaction spread across her face, and went back out to the front.

Skye smiled. Adaire might be in a human body, but apparently Jenny wasn't fooled. Was it her height? She'd have to ask Jenny later.

She took the mug of tea back into her room.

Adaire hadn't moved. But she was breathing more slowly, less panicked.

She held out the mug to Adaire, who took it, wrapping her hands around it as if she was freezing.

Skye pulled up another wooden chair and sat down, crossing her legs. Waiting.

Adaire sipped the tea, but said nothing for a time.

Finally, she looked at Skye with eyes that were filled with pain and worry.

"I don't know how to explain. It's awful."

"Take your time."

"It started just before I spoke to you last. The trees and shrubs at the Trust, the garden I was working at, were unhappy. Moisture seeping up in places it never had been before. The plants' roots were drowning. Trees which had grown there for hundreds upon hundreds of years. Oaks, hollies, yews. Ancient trees. Old souls. No one could say what caused the water to rise. Specialists were brought in to drain the land. It didn't work. The water table is rising, even far inland. And there's nowhere to drain the water to. They're all dying. Except the few water-loving plants."

Skye nodded and touched Adaire's arm.

"I'm sorry."

"But that's not the end of it. I was being stalked at work."

"Stalked."

"Hunted."

"By whom? Or what?"

"I don't know. It was subtle at first. I felt a presence. Watching me. Then I noticed it following me. It felt creepy."

"Human?"

"No, not human and not Fae either. I felt awful. Unable to help save the trees and like I was prey. So, yesterday the thing was following me. It's dark and dangerous, means me harm. I couldn't take it any more. I just fell apart. I took the shuttle back into town at the end of the day, went to my flat, gathered all my belongings and got on the first train here. I don't know if it followed me or not. I haven't been this afraid since we were imprisoned." Adaire looked at her, eyes filled with fear and pain.

Skye sighed deeply.

"I understand. I've felt it lately too. I went to Faerie and on the way back I felt like something was hunting me as well. It's terrifying."

Adaire sipped more tea.

"I don't know what to do, but I can't go back. I'm of no use to the trees. And I wonder if whatever's been stalking me caused the water to rise."

"Was it a Fomorian?" asked Skye.

"How could it be? They're all in the vault beneath Faerie."

"Not all of them."

"What do you mean?"

Skye told her about the Fomorian who'd been coming to the shop. And Meredith's suspicions that they had only caught the original Fomorians. That there were offspring.

Adaire said, "Then there's no hope, is there? Faerie will die and we will die with her."

Skye sat and looked at the dryad. Even in a human body, she didn't look normal. Or healthy. Then she saw the shadow of it.

"Adaire, you're not thinking clearly. You've got a fog of despair wrapped around you. Here, put the tea down and stand up."

Adaire did as she was told. Skye walked around her and searched for a way into the layer of despair. She could see its shadow clearly now. When she touched it, the shadow clung closer to Adaire almost as if it was a living thing.

Skye went to the cabinet and opened the drawer. She pulled out two candles and set them in holders and lit them. The she got out the cinnamon, lavender and jasmine incense and lit a stick, carrying it around the room. Letting the smoke curl around Adaire.

Then she set the incense in the holder.

"I want you to go deep inside yourself. Find your strength. Pull it up. When I say go, I want you to push your power outward. Can you feel the shadow wrapped around you?"

"Is that what it is?"

"Yes. It's not you, but it has attached itself to you. I want you to push outward at it. Making it release itself. Don't worry, I'll help. Now go find your strength. Deep inside."

Skye watched Adaire close her eyes and go within.

Skye sensed Aidan's presence and silently called out to him.

"Where are you?"

"Waiting in the back room of the store, in the back corner."

"I'm going to toss you something in a minute. Burn it please."

"My pleasure."

Skye focused herself on Adaire again.

After a time, she saw Adaire's face spark with surprise.

"Go," said Skye. "Push outward."

Skye found an opening and began to peel the shadow off. It had little claws and had dug itself into Adaire's human body. Skye continued to peel it off, forcing it to retract its claws. It was really nasty and mean. Eventually, she had the entire thing pulled off. She envisioned wadding it into a small ball. It snarled at her and bit. She bit back, tasting bitter blackness. Finally, she got it rolled up and then threw it through the wall to Aidan who incinerated the thing midair.

Skye took a deep breath to clear herself of the thing and then went to work again on Adaire. Beaming white light at her, helping the dryad heal herself. To heal the invisible wounds in her Fae and human bodies.

When Adaire was finished, she opened her eyes.

"You can sit down now and finish your tea."

"What was that?" asked Adaire.

"I call them shadows. I find them sometimes on human, especially on powerful humans. This one was particularly evil. It was siphoning off your Fae power and was fat and happy. You let it into your body and your psyche, though. Your despair gave it access."

"Crimey. I won't let that happen again."

"Feel better?"

"Yes, thank you." Adaire sat down and sipped her tea.

"Aidan's here. I don't know if you know him. A fire spirit. And Meredith is sending someone to guard you. A little late, I'd guess. You should stay here, in Glastonbury."

"I want to go back to Faerie, but I'm afraid to cross over the sea."

"So stay here. I'm going to find a larger place to live. We can all share it."

Adaire let out a deep breath.

"All right. I don't know how long I'll be able to tolerate a fire spirit though."

"He has better control than Egan. And you traveled with Egan for quite a while."

"I'll try it."

"Okay, then let's go find a safe place to live."

Although Skye wasn't sure that a safe place for Fae really existed anymore.

Chapter 19 ~ Clare

Clare unlocked the store, then closed and locked the door behind her. She blew on her frozen fingers, hot breath passing between the stitches of the knitted gloves. It didn't help much.

She switched the lights on in the back and looked.

It had been a week since All Hallow's Eve and she still checked every morning. But there had been no puddles of water, no Nag Champa. There wasn't today either. Everything was just as she left it. Except for the lingering earthy scent of burnt sage. Some of the displays had been rearranged. Jenny. She always liked to keep busy.

Clare took a deep breath, relaxing and turned the heat on.

Pirate mewed at her from inside the office. Clare turned off the alarm and unlocked the door.

Pirate was sitting up inside the cardboard box.

"Good morning honey. I'll get you some food and fresh water." She stroked the cat, feeling the softness of her fur. A good diet had done wonders for her coat in just a short time.

The kittens were wiggling around a bit more now. Their eyes were beginning to open, but she knew they couldn't see well yet. The black one's eyes had opened yesterday and it seemed to be moving around more than the others.

Clare did her morning chores. Jenny arrived just as it was time to unlock the store.

"Good morning," said Jenny. "It's so cold out this morning!" She pulled her coat closer to her.

"It is, but I've got the heat cranked up in here. It should be toasty in no time."

Clare went to the back and poured herself a cup of tea from the teapot. She sipped the harsh black tea mingled with rich cream. It balanced her. Set her up for the day.

Jenny came to the hallway and slipped out of her coat, but looked as if she didn't want to. Then she went back out front.

Jenny scurried around the store. Tidying up and rearranging things. She always had such energy in the mornings.

Clare was waiting for the smelly office to air out a bit before she went in to work on the computer. She went out to the cash register and found the stash of opened incense that the staff burned in the store.

Clare chose crabapple. She knew it wouldn't smell like crabapples, but it would provide a bite that some of the overly floral incenses didn't have. It would be perfect for this bitterly cold winter day.

She lit the stick and walked around the store, the back and the office, twice, waving it around, distributing the smoke and cleansing the entire building.

She had work to do today and needed clarity.

Then she set the incense in a holder and put it in the hallway. Close enough to keep clearing the smell out of the office, but not so close she'd choke on too much smoke.

Clare picked up her tea and went into the office. She switched on the computer and waited. Today was the day she would announce the event schedule.

Since the ritual, people who wanted to give a talk or teach a workshop had come out of the hedgerows. Anyone who'd ever written a metaphysical book and lived in England, and a few that didn't live here, wanted to speak or give a workshop.

Where had they all come from? Tarot readers, witches, wizards, shamans, fantasy artists, psychics, druids, astrologers, crystal healers, face readers, self help writers and so many more. She could book one of them every day for the next six months and still have people left over.

It took a couple of hours, but she finally had a schedule for the next three months. Clare gave preference to speakers she'd actually met and knew would be good. Then to people whose work she was familiar with. When she finished, the store was booked three nights a week and one, sometimes two weekend days, if a workshop needed to be two days long.

She really would need to hire another person or Jenny and Marcella would revolt.

Clare got up from the desk and stretched. She watched the kittens' clumsy attempts at movement. They were crawling, as best they could, inside the giant cardboard box.

Maybe next week she'd change out the blanket that lined it. She still didn't want to disturb them or Pirate. They'd doubled in size in the week since they'd been born. Their ears had unfolded and looked more normal now.

Clare got another cup of tea and peered out into the front.

Jenny was talking with a customer about some jewelry. The sun gleamed in through the large windows, making the crystals shine.

Clare went back into the office.

She still had to plan the open house. Which needed to happen in two weeks, prime holiday shopping time.

She'd asked Kristin to come and do a presentation on making fairy houses at the open house. Malcolm, the man who provided the store with the beautiful drums he made and painted, was doing a drum painting workshop. She needed to order food and drinks, buy seasonal decorations for the store, and have Marcella and Jenny decorate.

This would be her first Yule, Winter Solstice and Christmas with the shop. She was really looking forward to it.

She designed an invitation to the open house. It would be included in the email to the store's mailing list, along with the event schedule and a discount coupon for November.

Clare finished up both, adding some pretty fiddly bits. Then printed copies of the calendar and the open house for the front door and to give out to customers.

She took the copies out front and set the two piles on the glass counter near the cash register. Then took one of each and taped them to the door window.

Jenny looked at the piles on the counter and asked, "We're going to be open three nights a week?"

"Yeah," said Clare. "We need to get people used to us having events in the evening."

Jenny frowned.

"What?" asked Clare, softly.

"Who's going to be working those nights?"

Clare said, "Well, I will, if no one else. I know neither you or Marcella are thrilled about it. I'd love it if you'd each be willing to take one night a week. After a couple of weeks, if things are going well and we're selling things, I'll be able to hire another person. I'm really trying to grow this store. This time of year is also our high season, but this time it's for the locals, not just for tourists. Even though some will come to the village on their holiday. I'm also trying to build community. To let people know we're here for them. I think we need others the most in the deep darkness of winter."

The words flowed out of her mouth as if they'd come from somewhere else other than her brain.

As if they were magic.

Jenny raised her eyebrows and said, "I can do one night a week. A little extra money for Christmas wouldn't hurt. Maybe the boys can go hang out with Mum those nights. Do them all some good to spend some time with each other."

"And it'll give people a chance to see those adorable kittens. Which might mean we'll find good homes for all of them," said Clare

"About that," said Jenny. "I have a friend who lost her cat a month ago. She's been heartbroken. I've been waiting till they were old enough to be handled, and she's ready to think about a new companion. I wanted to bring her by."

"Certainly," said Clare. "Guess I'll need to decide which one I want, huh?"

"You're taking one?" asked Jenny.

"Yes. I thought Pirate could use some company here all alone at night."

"Lovely. Do you know which one you want?"

"Not a clue," said Clare. "They're all so precious. I just haven't been able to decide."

"You'll figure it out."

"Well, I'd better go get those newsletters out," Clare said and walked into the back.

She'd thought Jenny would object to working nights. It was a relief that she'd agreed to one night a week.

Clare loaded everything into her newsletter email service and sent it out to the entire email list with the push of one button. How wonderful was that? Sometimes, she loved technology.

The effect of getting so much done felt very freeing.

She was stepping into her new role, her new life. Even more so than opening the store. After working in retail for more than a decade, she'd already known how to do that.

This felt completely different. This was stepping into a dark tunnel without a light and hoping she could come out alive at the other end.

Chapter 20 ~ Skye

The three of them were able to rent a small furnished cottage. The furniture was old and unmatched, but the place was cozy and had enough bedrooms. Although Adaire's had nothing in it, but an ancient beat-up desk whose various layers of paint showed through.

There weren't enough beds, they'd have to find another one for Adaire. But Adaire said she was fine with sleeping on the huge maroon couch for a few nights until that was possible.

The place had wood floors and the old radiators overheated the cottage, but it was quaint. The cottage sat on a large lot at one end of town, surrounded by other houses. It was just a short walk to the shop.

It felt safe, which was what Adaire had wanted. What they all wanted.

Skye had to put down a huge cash deposit, since she didn't have a bank account or a normal job. But the landlord knew

Clare and her store. Skye suspected that the woman let a few things slide that most landlords wouldn't.

Skye sat at the wooden kitchen table in her thin purple tunic and purple leggings. She wore brown leather boots over wool socks. Her hair braided back into one thick plait.

Her fingers wrapped around a cup of hot mint tea, she inhaled the heat. The minty moistness took her back to summer.

She looked out the window at the dismal back garden. The last tenant had a vegetable garden. But they'd been gone for two months and the plants had turned to a brown pulpy mess as winter approached. The trees nearby were mostly bare. Everything looked gray and dreary out there today.

Adaire came into the room, glanced out the window and said, "I've been meaning to do something about that."

"What?" asked Skye.

"The debris needs to be gathered together and composted. The beds tidied up and then covered with mulch for the winter. It's really too late to plant any vegetables or even a green manure. But I could still make it look nicer."

"So why haven't you gotten out there?" asked Skye.

"I'm still feeling a little uneasy."

"About being hunted?"

Adaire nodded.

"Maybe Aidan could go out with you while I'm working. Make you feel safer."

"Maybe. He doesn't make me feel particularly safe."

Skye looked at her questioningly.

"It's a fire thing," said Adaire.

Skye nodded. Fire and plant elementals had problems together. So did fire and water. The only spirits who really got along with fire were air and stone. Which was why so much of Faerie had been irritated when Egan became Luminary. But fire had been what Faerie needed to survive the boundaries falling and the attack of the Formorians.

Adaire got a glass of water and sat down at the table with her. She sat looking directly out the window, Skye sat sideways.

"How long will you be staying here?" asked Adaire.

"I don't know. I'd originally planned to stay for a very long time. My task is to help acclimate humans to the idea of Faerie. To let them know that Fae are all around them. It's going to take years, decades. But now I don't know. Meredith suspects Faerie will have to be closed again."

Adaire nodded. "I'm feeling anxious. I want to be doing my work. Helping trees. But I can't. I don't like this trapped feeling."

"What did you do before you were trapped by the Fomorians? Out in the human world?"

"I was a garden coach. I helped people take the garden they had and turn it into what they wanted and could handle."

"Where?"

"In Seattle."

"So, a similar climate to here?"

"Yes."

"Why don't you turn this garden into a lovely garden? Plant some trees and bushes and stuff. Then, as people notice, word will spread. Do the same thing here as you did in Seattle. Help people create gardens."

"I don't know the area. I don't know the nurseries. And I'm afraid to leave the house."

"Take Aidan with you, until someone else comes from Faerie. Grow stronger."

Adaire stared at her and Skye knew she had directly hit the problem.

"You're right. I've grown weak. I've let them win, haven't I?"

"They've not won yet, but yes, you've grown weak and afraid. It happens. Now that you can see it, what will you do about it?"

"I guess I'll do what I do best. Help things grow. This garden could use a couple of small trees. And perhaps one large one."

"Good. Well, I'd better get moving," said Skye, finishing the last of her tea and getting up to swish out the cup in the sink. Its minty flavor made her mouth tingle. "After Aidan walks me to the shop, I'll have him come back and pick you up. You can go find nurseries."

Adaire was staring out the window. Skye knew she was calculating how many plants could happily fit and where.

She got some cash out of her wallet and left it on the kitchen table.

"That's all I've got for now. I'll have more later today, but we'll need that for food. These human bodies need to be fed."

She'd need to add in another day to her schedule because now she was supporting three people. Soon there would be a fourth. Luckily, the clients were there.

After Skye dressed, she walked with Aidan to the store. The wind blew her hair around and she swirled in circles with it, laughing. It was chilly, but not biting. A normal winter wind.

Outside the shop, she kissed him goodbye and he turned, smiling, to walk back to the cottage.

She went inside the warm store, and although her cheeks were cold, Skye felt alive and ready to get to work. Her first client would come in about thirty minutes.

Marcella was at the cash register ringing up a customer.

Skye waved and walked into the back. Clare was in the office, standing over the box of kittens.

Skye said, "Good morning."

"Oh, hello. How are you?"

"I'm grand and you?"

"Good. I'm good. Trying to decide which kitten to keep, so other people can choose."

Skye went into the office. She hadn't had time to really even look at the kittens. She squatted and petted Pirate on the head. The cat began to purr loudly.

Then she looked at each one of the kittens, picking it up and petting it. Getting each one to purr. Telling it how beautiful it was.

"Which ones do you like the best?" asked Skye.

Clare squatted down next to her.

"That's the trouble. I don't know. I like them all. I can't keep them all. Two cats is enough in this space."

Skye nodded and said, "Well, this orange guy, he's going to be the most outgoing. This black one, she's very shy, she'd be better in a quiet house, maybe with someone older and quieter, no kids. This tortoiseshell, she's got an attitude. She wants to be an only cat, but with a person to push around. This sleek gray guy, he wants to hunt. He needs space to get outdoors. The white one, well, she's a good choice too. Not quite as outgoing as the orange though. The gray tabby, she's also a hunter."

Skye shrugged, "Those are my thoughts."

Clare said, "Thank you for narrowing it down for me. That'll help me find homes for the others. How did you do that? The vet said we wouldn't even be able to tell their gender for weeks."

"It's a Fae thing. I looked into their possible futures. Saw who they could become."

"Possible futures?" asked Clare.

"We all have many possible futures and they're all intertwined. This orange kitten could become outgoing, loving and trusting everyone. If someone adopted him who abused him, he could become mean. The little black one could be a loving and trusting companion, or in a noisy household that continually overruled her requests for food, love and solitude, she could become withdrawn and skittish. Always afraid."

"Just like humans," said Clare.

"We are all more alike than we are different."

Clare nodded, still staring at the kittens.

Skye stood and said, "Well, I'd better go get my room ready. I've got a client coming soon.

She went to her room in the back and unlocked the door. The room smelled of the vanilla scent she'd used last. Skye turned the ceiling light on and hung up her coat and bag. She switched the heater on and tidied everything up. Turned on the massage table warmer.

Then she put her mobile in the music system and decided on some Gregorian chant. She put more vanilla oil in the diffuser, lighting the candle beneath it, turned on the two table lamps and switched off the ceiling lamp. Skye sat on one of the wooden chairs and removed her boots and socks, putting them beneath the chair.

She sat cross legged in the chair and grounded herself, feeling her energy sink deep in the earth beneath the store. Then she began to breathe deeply, focusing on relaxing herself, so she could be open to what her new client might need.

She glanced at the clock and put her feet on the floor. Then got up and opened the door and closed it behind her to keep the room warm. She went out towards the front.

Clare was still standing in front of the kittens.

"Is everything okay?" asked Skye.

"Is it crazy that I want them all?"

"No, but do you have space for them? Sometimes we want more than is actually good for us. Life puts limits on us from all directions. Time, money, space, energy. So we have to make decisions."

"Yeah. Deciding. That's what I'm having a hard time with."

"You could take two to live at your house and another one for the store."

"I've been thinking about that. Keeping the orange guy for the store and taking the black one and the white one home. I could use some company at home. But they'd need to be indoor cats. I live too close to a busy street."

Skye knelt down and put her hands on the black one and the white one. She asked their souls if they would be okay living inside and together, with Clare.

She smiled.

"These two would be perfectly happy indoors. You'll need to get them things to climb on. And cat toys. Wow. What a change that will be for you. To have two babies. And you know, kittens are nocturnal."

Clare smiled.

The bell on the front door clinked and Skye went out to the counter. A tall woman, huddled in a wool coat, scarf and gloves had come in and looked hesitantly at her.

"I'm looking for Skye."

"I'm Skye. Are you Marlena?"

"Yes."

"Well, come on back. I've got the room warming up."

Marlena followed her to the back and Skye opened the door.

The vanilla scent was quite strong. Skye blew out the candle beneath the diffuser.

"Oh, this is wonderful. It's toasty in here."

"The heat helps people's muscles relax. Have a seat."

Marlena sat and Skye pulled up another wooden chair.

Skye explained how she worked and eventually Marlena took off her gloves and unbuttoned her coat, but didn't take it off.

The woman had scars covering both hands, but she didn't try to hide them. They looked patchy. Burn scars of some sort?

"What can I do for you?" asked Skye.

"I've been having a lot of pain in my ribs. Feeling like I can't breathe."

"Have you been to a doctor?"

Marlena said, "Yes. She said it's anxiety, not asthma. And she wants to put me on medication. I told her I'd think about it. I've been under a lot of stress lately. That'll go away, I hope."

"What's going to make it go away?" asked Skye.

"My sister was killed in an accident last month. I've been dealing with all her belongings, tying up the loose ends of her life and trying to console my parents. Because my brother's too busy to come help."

"So, you're having to be the strong one. And there's no time for you to grieve."

"Exactly."

"And you're also angry about it."

"That too."

"Do you have anyone to lean on?"

"No, I'm single. Alone."

"Okay, I'll see what I can do for you. You're carrying a lot of stuff. Time to release as much of it as you can. I'll go outside for about five minutes and you can undress and get under the sheet. I'll knock before I come in and we can get to work."

Marlena nodded.

Skye got up and left the room, closing the door behind her.

She went to the hallway and lifted the teapot, testing it. Thankfully, there was some left. She poured it into a cup, then added a bit of water to cool it. She sipped the bitter black tea.

This was going to take some work.

Marlena's grief and anger were palpable. They seemed woven deep into her soul. Skye wasn't sure how much she'd be able to loosen up. The woman was attached to being angry.

At least she could help somewhat. Lower Marlena's anxiety level enough so she could breathe.

After five minutes, Skye rinsed out the empty mug, filled it with water and took it back to her room. She knocked and went in. Marlena was stretched out on the massage table.

"I love this heat," she said. "And the music."

"Good. I forgot to ask about the music."

Skye set the mug down on a coaster and opened a drawer, taking out a bottle of massage oil. Squirted some of the palm of one hand, then rubbed her hands together.

"I'll start on your back," said Skye.

Chapter 21 ⚜ Clare

Clare stood at the counter. It was Saturday and she was the only one in the store. Skye had taken the day off from appointments. Jenny had taken her boys to their games. It was a good day for it. Crisp and windy. Marcella was off to Bristol, Christmas shopping with friends.

It would be a quiet day until one. Raven was giving a tarot reading workshop. Seven people had signed up. More might drop in.

Clare had just restocked all the tarot decks, making a special display of six brand new ones. Many people collected the cards for their artwork. She loved collectors, they always wanted to buy something new.

She stood sipping her oolong tea. The slightly floral taste rolled around her mouth.

She'd gotten everything done already. Office cleaned up from the cats, cash register ready to go. She'd put on some

Anuna on the sound system and was listening to the beautiful voices twirl around each other, doing aural acrobatics.

The shop was clean and perfect. Not a thing she should be doing. Which almost never happened.

Time to relax. She sipped more tea and closed her eyes. She could actually read something.

Clare was just about to grab a book off the shelf when there was a thumping noise coming from the back. She went to the office and opened the door.

The all gray kitten had managed to get out of the box. Pirate was lying down nursing all the others. Maybe the gray one had climbed on top of her and gotten out.

It began mewing and Clare picked him up, petted him and put him in the box.

"Not yet, my friend. You're far too young to go exploring."

Before she left tonight, she'd need to move everyone to the taller box she'd found. That way they could get new, clean bedding, too.

The bell on the front door rang as it opened. Clare shut the office door, just in case someone else managed to get out of the box while she was busy.

She went out to the front of the store.

A tall, slender man had just come in.

Clare's breath caught.

He had long, wavy dark hair with a few gray streaks. He looked to be in his forties, maybe older. Dressed in new jeans, old boots and wearing a reddish brown leather jacket. The man had a groundedness about him that made her like him immediately.

He was easily the most striking man she'd ever seen. Sharp cheekbones and warm gray eyes. Around his mouth lay lines etched in his skin from smiling often.

"Good morning," said Clare, trying to regain her equilibrium.

"Morning," he said, giving a short bow.

That made her smile. His accent was soft, somewhere in Ireland, west coast perhaps?

He didn't act like a normal customer. He looked around as if bewildered.

"Can I help you find something?" she asked.

"Actually, I was told I could find Skye here."

"She's not in today."

"Oh," he said, looking completely lost.

"Would you like to leave a message for the next time she comes in?"

"I don't know. I've come a long ways. I need to get hold of her soon." He seemed distressed.

"What's your name. I'll try to call her." She was stalling, trying to keep him around. When was the last time she'd found a guy even half this good looking?

"I'm Fiachna."

"I'm Clare," she extended her hand and he hesitated, then took her hand, not shaking it, just holding it.

She shook his large warm hand, then reluctantly let go.

It was then that the suspicion hit her.

Clare pulled out her mobile and called Skye.

Fiachna went over to the crystals and began examining them.

"Hello," said Skye.

"Skye, there's a gentleman here to see you. His name's Fiachna and he said he needed to talk to you today."

"Fiachna! He's there? Can you put him on?" asked Skye, clearly excited.

Clare said, "Fiachna, Skye wants to speak with you."

She handed him the mobile and he looked at it suspiciously.

"You put it up to your ear, like this," said Clare, showing him.

He took the mobile and copied her. His face lit up when he heard Skye's voice.

Fae.

Didn't know how to shake hands or use a mobile.

She watched him as he listened to Skye and occasionally said a few words.

Clare pretended to rearrange the display of new books on the counter, while she watched him.

Like Skye, he'd made a lovely human body. What did he really look like?

After a time, he handed the mobile back to her.

"Skye wants to talk to you," he said, softly.

"Hello," said Clare.

"Clare, I have a huge favor to ask you."

"Sure."

"Fiachna is new here. He's a little disoriented and perhaps frightened. He's not used to humans or villages. I'm far over on the coast helping Adaire buy plants. I can't get back till this evening. Could you let Fiachna into my room? I told him perhaps he could hang out there. I can come collect him as soon as I get back to town. He's the most trustworthy Fae I've ever known. You can trust him alone in the store. If you leave directions I can turn the alarm on after I pick him up."

"I'm sure that would be fine," said Clare. "I'll leave the directions for you. How about if I tape them to your door?"

"Perfect. Thank you so much. I can't tell you how much I appreciate it."

"It's no problem. Really."

Clare hung up and slipped her mobile back into her trouser pocket.

"You're welcome to stay. You don't have to hang out in Skye's room, but I'll unlock the door for you. Come on back."

"Thank you," he said. "You are very kind."

"Where are you from?" she asked.

"Ireland."

"How did you come over?"

"I walked."

"On water?" she asked, unlocking Skye's door and turning on the overhead light.

"Beneath," he said. Then he looked confused. "Humans can't do that, can they?"

"No," she said. "But I already knew you were Fae."

He raised his eyebrows. "How?"

"You created a perfectly beautiful human body. You don't know how to shake hands or use a mobile."

His laugh was warm and sounded like he did it often.

"I thought Skye would be here. That I would not really have to interact with humans, I could learn how later. I did not need to make a human body. This is what I really look like. I do not usually wear human clothes like these though. Meredith insisted I find some after I left the water."

Clare wasn't going to ask what he did to find them. "Skye usually takes weekends off."

"Weekends. There's so much about humans I do not understand."

The bell rang on the front door.

"I have a customer. You can stay in here or come out. I'll go see what they want. If you want to, feel free to close the door."

He smiled at her and she turned and went back out to the front.

Wow. What she wouldn't do to keep that warm smile around permanently.

She walked past the office, stopping in the hallway and grabbing her mug of tea from the counter, sipping the creamy, but now cold liquid.

What was she thinking? She had no idea who he was. He could be gone tomorrow. He probably already had someone. Clare might be mildly attractive to a human, but to a Fae…

Raven was coming towards her carrying a large box of supplies.

"Hi," she said. "I came early so I'd have time to set up before lunch."

"Perfect. What do you need?" said Clare returning to the back of the building with her. Walking past Skye's door, she saw it was still open, but didn't see Fiachna.

"I think a large table and chairs, maybe two tables. Some of the older ladies who came to the Samhain ritual pointed out that it's hard for them to get up and down off the floor these days."

Clare hadn't even considered that. Another thing to work out before the next ritual.

Raven put her box down on a wooden chair.

She and Raven got out a large folding table and set it up. Then they moved the large wooden table from the corner and put them together so they formed one square table in the middle of the back area.

Raven pulled a large green cloth out of her box and they spread it over the tables.

"Perfect," said Raven.

Buy a couple of tablecloths, Clare added to her mental list. Not everyone would be as well prepared as Raven.

Raven began pulling things out of her box, while Clare collected chairs from around the room and put them in place. She had eight. If someone dropped in, there wouldn't be enough.

Clare got the two extra wooden chairs from the office, leaving just her rolling desk chair. She carried them to the back, setting them against the wall.

She'd been going to the antique shops buying up any inexpensive wooden chairs. They'd need a lot more for all the upcoming events. Ten more were coming from Gregory's shop, early in the week. But she'd need more than that. She didn't want plastic or metal folding chairs, but it might have to happen. Wood was so much nicer.

Raven was setting up. Clare made another pot of tea. She needed to get something larger to serve beverages at the events. Maybe a dispenser for filtered water. Hot and cold. Then people could make tea.

She should set it up in the front of the shop, so regular customers could have it too. She needed to figure all that out. Jenny would know what to do. She was a household goddess.

Skye's door was still open, Clare went to it, making a lot of noise.

Fiachna was lying on the small rug in the far corner of the room. Seemingly sound asleep. Clare quietly pulled the door almost closed and turned off the lights. She'd been about to close the door, when she realized he might not know how to open a doorknob.

Did they even have doors in Faerie? She'd have to ask.

Clare peeked in the office, checking to make sure all the kittens were still where they should be. Everyone was sleeping. She closed the door and went back out to the counter and began making lists of things to buy and do before the open house, which was only a week away.

Chapter 22 ~ Skye

Skye, Adaire and Aidan made it back to the shop long after dark. It had been a long walk from the nursery and Skye's human body ached. It hadn't walked that far ever.

But Adaire was happy and filled with plans for the new garden. The plants would be delivered on Monday.

Skye unlocked the front door of the shop and the others followed her in. It was dark except for the twinkle lights Clare had in the front window, but they cast enough light to see by.

The only sounds were the kittens mewing and hissing. The shop smelled of sandalwood.

They walked into the back and almost tripped over Fiachna sitting in the hallway, just outside the office. The office door was open and he was sitting in the dark, watching the kittens play. It seemed like they'd just begun moving yesterday.

He stood quickly when they came around the counter. Skye hugged him and said, "It's so good to see you."

His hug was strong and firm.

Adaire hugged him too.

"I am here to protect you," Fiachna said.

"I'm so pleased you're here," Adaire said.

"Are you okay?" asked Skye.

Fiachna said, "I am fine. I was just very, very tired. I was overwhelmed by the human world. It is very strange. I have only seen humans on the boundaries of Faerie. I never spoke to them. I did not know about shaking hands. Clare caught me out."

"Well, she knows we're all Fae and she met Dylan and Meredith, too. So, she probably guessed when you wanted to talk to me," said Skye.

"She is very smart and the soul of graciousness," said Fiachna.

"Yes, she is," said Aidan.

Skye went to back to her room, closed, then locked the door and pulled the alarm instructions Clare had left for her off the door. Skye went back to the office.

"Shall we go?"

Fiachna looked at the kittens.

"They'll be fine. You can come visit them again," said Skye.

"I like it here. The amount of energy that passes through is reviving. It feels very much like home. All the stones."

"Energy. Oh, you mean the ley lines." Then Skye asked "What stones?"

Fiachna pointed to the displays of crystals.

"Oh," she said.

Fiachna didn't seem to want to leave. Interesting.

"I'm starving," said Adaire. "And this body's tired. We should go."

Fiachna nodded.

Her stomach was growling too. They'd hurried back as fast as they could, to get Fiachna, hadn't stopped for food.

Skye closed the door to the office. Did Clare normally lock it? Probably. She opened the door and pushed in the lock on the other side. Then pulled it closed again.

The others went out front while she set the alarm, then they left the store and she locked the front door.

The walk to their cottage was nothing compared to the hike to and from the nursery.

It was cold for their human bodies though.

By the time they got home, Skye's fingers felt frozen. She turned the heat on immediately.

They took coats off and Aidan made mint tea. Adaire pulled leftover roast beef, bread and condiments out of the refrigerator and made sandwiches.

Skye noticed Fiachna seemed distant.

He told them Egan was preparing for war with the Fomorians offspring.

"Baby Fomorians is what he calls them, which make Meredith angry," said Fiachna.

"Why?" asked Adaire.

"She thinks he underestimates them. It is his way of allaying his fear of them. To mock them," said Fiachna. "He is also unhappy about Lassair returning to her village."

"Why doesn't he go after her?" asked Skye.

Fiachna shrugged. "Too busy? Too afraid?"

"Wouldn't stop me," said Aidan.

"Me neither," said Fiachna.

"Has Dylan returned to Faerie?" asked Skye.

"He arrived shortly before I left. He followed the Fomorian who had been coming to Clare's shop back to the depths of the sea. Apparently that one has been gathering others. He was on land trying to find other Fomorians who were not from the water. The other water Fomorians, he had already gathered."

"He hasn't returned to Clare's shop, whatever that means," said Skye.

She sipped her tea.

"That is good," said Fiachna. "I would not want her to get hurt. She has the golden speech."

Aidan looked up from his sandwich at that. Skye watched him.

"What does that mean?" asked Adaire.

"Those with the gift of golden speech have the ability to call others to action. To persuade them to the person's cause. It is a gift few Fae have. I have never heard of it in a human, but then it has been long since Faerie intermingled with humans."

"So that means Clare is part Fae?" asked Skye.

"Perhaps, far back in her bloodline. Or perhaps humans have the gift as well," said Fiachna.

Aidan asked, "Where does Egan plan to wage this war?"

"I do not know," said Fiachna. "I did not ask. I knew I was coming here instead."

"I should be there," said Aidan.

A wave of fear passed through Skye. She didn't want Aidan to leave, especially to go to war. Faerie hadn't been at war in her lifetime, but she remembered the old stories.

She said, "You're a healer. Are you a warrior as well?"

"The two go hand in hand. Warriors always need healers."

"I can't go," she said. "I'm too afraid."

Adaire said, "Oh course you can't go. Your work is here. No one is asking you to go, Skye."

Skye didn't miss the glare that the dryad shot at Aidan.

Fiachna said to Aidan, "If you really feel that you need to go, I will guard both Adaire and Skye until someone else can be sent over."

Aidan said, "Thank you. I'll need to think on what I should do."

After they finished feeding their human bodies, the Skye, Aidan and Adaire put the bodies to bed, slipping out of them. Fiachna looked human enough to pass. Stone Fae always looked more human, which was why he'd spent millennia guarding and walking the boundaries of Faerie.

Adaire, Skye and Fiachna sat and talked while Aidan sat, staring out the window into the darkness.

Before dawn came, it was clear Aidan had made a decision. He went into the bedroom and began packing a few clothes.

Skye felt heavy with grief. She didn't want to lose him. Finding a lover was such a rare thing for her and had been for a couple thousand years. Ever since she'd left Faerie.

She dug through her wallet, pulling out a wad of cash.

"Here, you'll need this for the passage."

"I can't go legally, you know. No papers."

"I know, which means you'll need more than just passage fare for a ferry. You'll have to pay someone more than that to illegally take you over."

"Thank you," he said, bowing, suddenly formal.

"I'll miss you," she said.

"I'm coming back. You know that."

"No, I don't know that. Life has no certainty anymore." With Egan planning for a war, any future looked bleak.

"Believe that I'll come back to you," he said, putting his hands on her upper arms.

"I'll try."

"Is there anything that would help you believe?"

"No. Your fate isn't in your control. Not in war, not even in everyday life."

"So you don't doubt the love I feel for you, it's my ability to overcome a Fomorian?"

"An army of Fomorians."

"Well, whether you believe it or not, I will return to you," he said.

They kissed and made love as Fae one last time.

Then he slipped back into his human body and left the house.

Skye longed to fly away. To feel the rush of cold air on her face and to move through the clouds with only her wings.

But she felt too afraid.

Instead she slid into her human body and lost herself in sleep and dreams of flying.

Chapter 23 ⚜ Clare

Clare lit a lavender candle near the cash register. The days were passing at an alarming rate. She kept trying to calm herself.

It wasn't working.

The open house was tomorrow and she wasn't ready yet.

She breathed in the lavender scent, willing it to ease her anxiety. There was a crashing sound from the office. She groaned.

Clare went into the back and opened the office door. Her desk lamp was on the floor, but luckily, the bulb wasn't broken. She put it back on top of the desk and picked up the orange guy, who was huddled beneath the desk.

"Oh, I can see you're going to be trouble aren't you? Maybe that would be a good name for you." She snuggled with him, until he began purring. He was so soft and smelled fresh. She rubbed her face on his fur and he purred louder.

Jenny came back and said, "What happened?"

"Desk lamp. This is only going to get worse, huh?"

"Yes. But in another two, three weeks you can wean them and they can find new homes."

"That soon?" asked Clare.

"Kittenhood is really short. Well, at least the part where they need Mom."

Pirate jumped out of the box and went out to the front of the store. She climbed into the front window and sat in the display.

"Well, I guess she needs a break from the little monsters," said Jenny, laughing.

Clare put the now squirming orange kitten down inside the box.

"Now, stay in the box. I need to baby-proof the office if I'm going to leave them in here at night."

"Good idea. So, I finished putting the shipment of books out. What next?"

"Jewelry. A whole bunch came in yesterday. I opened the box and made sure everything was there, but I haven't put any of it out. So put a selection of it up where there's room. The box is in the back."

Jenny went towards the back storage shelves.

"Ooh, more candles, too," Jenny yelled.

"We got three deliveries yesterday. I hope we get the other boxes today in time to put them out."

Clare sat at the desk and went over her checklist.

The next thing on her list was to call Kristin. Her message machine answered.

"Hi Kristin, this is Clare. Just wanted to make sure I've got everything you need for tomorrow. I have the large tables and I wrapped them with a roll of butcher paper, like you suggested. All set up there. I'll have the ceiling lights on, so the lighting will be good. We'll have lots of snacks and beverages going all day long. You told me you're bringing all the supplies, wood, glue, paint, moss, etc. Save your receipts and I'll pay for it. I think that's about it. If you want to bring stuff this afternoon and set up, please do. We'll be open till five. Otherwise, I'll see you tomorrow morning."

She checked that item off the list. She'd called Malcolm earlier today and made sure she had everything for his drum painting workshop tomorrow afternoon.

Tomorrow would be interesting, to see if she could host an open house, along with the two free workshops.

Free for guests, not for her. She was paying both Kristin and Malcolm to teach people. And paying for supplies, although if people wanted to paint a drum they either had to bring their own or buy one. Drums were expensive.

Skye walked past the door towards her room and said, "Hi, gotta hurry. Running late."

Fiachna was following her and stood in the office doorway.

"Good morning," he said, his deep, rich voice made her insides go all squishy.

"Well hello. I haven't seen you around much lately."

"I am helping Adaire make a garden at the cottage. Gardening has no end of work."

Clare laughed. "I know. I have a small, very neglected garden. I just don't have a lot of interest in it."

"Perhaps you should hire Adaire to make it what you want it to be. She makes beautiful gardens. Even I was surprised at what she has done with a bare, flat piece of land."

"Maybe I should. It would be nice to have a garden to sit in on the rare day off."

"You are spending too much time at work?"

"Right now I am. I hope to hire another person in a week. If that happens I can take more days off."

"That would be good. Humans work too much. Life is about more than just work."

"I know. The whole point of this shop is to help people find themselves, the deeper part of their beings."

"Is that how you humans do it? With pretty rocks and seer craft? I guess we Fae are different. We go out into nature to remind ourselves who we are and our place on this great Earth."

"Some humans do that too. Everyone's different. Some humans work and live in large cities. Those pretty rocks might be as close to nature as they get."

"Larger cities than this one?" he asked, a look of panic racing across his face.

"Much, much larger. With buildings that reach up into the sky. No trees, no plants, few animals."

He shook his head. "Humans have talked for eons about hell. I think that would be hell for me."

"Me too."

The white kitten leapt out of the box and Fiachna bent down and picked her up. She grabbed a hunk of his long hair with her little claws and began chewing on it.

He laughed.

Skye's client walked past, then backed up and waved at Clare. It was Emma.

Skye came back a couple of minutes later and poured herself a cup of tea.

"So," she said. "Everything all ready for tomorrow?"

Clare held up her to do list.

"I've got so much to do today. All the stuff I've been putting off. Thank goodness both Jenny and Marcella are here today. I just can't get focused. The kittens have become crazy monkeys today. All of a sudden they're all climbing and jumping out of the box. I need a kitten wrangler."

"Me, me, me. I want to be a kitten wrangler," said Marcella, walking past the office to the back, carrying large bags.

"I've already got plans for you dear."

"Well, I'm coming tomorrow," said Skye. "If I can help, let me know. And Adaire and Fiachna are coming too."

Fiachna nodded. He grabbed the black kitten just as she climbed out of the box and held her up next to the white kitten. The black one just looked around, wonder filling her eyes.

"How are you?" Clare asked Skye.

"I'm doing okay. I miss him, but gotta get on with my life."

Clare nodded as if she understood.

But she didn't.

She'd never had a lover. Never had time and it wasn't like men had ever been pounding down the door. She'd only been asked out once, in school. By a boy who repelled her with his aggressiveness.

"Well," said Skye, draining her tea. "time to get to work."

She went back to her room.

Fiachna put the two purring kittens back into the box, where the others were stalking and pouncing on each other. Meowing and hissing.

Clare sipped her black tea with cream. She'd skipped lunch and her stomach was roiling around. Unhappy from all the tea.

"I had better go back to the cottage to be there when Adaire needs my help."

He didn't look like he wanted to go. Just stood, mesmerized by the kittens' play.

"You're welcome to hang out here if you want."

What made her say that? She never wanted anyone to hang out while she was working. But Fiachna was different. He didn't need her to entertain him. He actually seemed quite self-sufficient. He seemed grounded, more solid, at least than most humans she knew. Then again, he wasn't human. She had to keep reminding herself of that.

Not that she needed to entertain anyone these days. The kittens were more than enough.

"Really?" he asked. "I would not want to disturb you. I know you have a lot of work to do."

"You won't disturb me. I'll just keep on with my list here."

"Okay. I would like to stay. Just a little longer. Then I truly must go help Adaire." He sat down on the wood floor next to the box and peered inside, smiling.

Clare went back to her list and actually made it through the entire thing: phone calls, emails and ordering. Every now and then she caught him watching her.

Then the delivery came and she had six boxes to unpack. Quietly. Because Skye had clients all afternoon.

Marcella and Jenny hung sparkly silver, white and blue snowflakes from the ceiling in the front of the store. Yesterday they'd put up the white and green fabric in the back, adding them to the scarlet which had been left hanging from Samhain. Skye hadn't been there, so Clare had chosen that day to decorate the back. No way to do that without noise.

The day before, the Christmas tree had been delivered. Clare had ordered a lot of Christmas ornaments to sell and used those to decorate the tree in the front of the store. She hoped all the ornaments would sell by the time the tree needed to be taken down.

And the kittens were definitely going to be confined to the back. Otherwise they'd have a great party with the tree. The whole store actually.

Somehow, she'd figure out how to keep them back there. Maybe she needed a cage for them.

Clare hadn't figured that one out.

Yet.

Chapter 24 ~ Skye

On the way to the shop for the open house, Skye stopped at the tea shop and bought a cinnamon bun for breakfast.

"That's disgusting," said Adaire.

"Yes it is. And I'm going to eat the whole thing."

Fiachna just smiled.

Skye ate a bit of it before she even left the shop. The sugary cinnamon taste filled her mouth. She loved the gooey texture.

They walked down the crowded street. Skye wore her big boots, jeans and winter coat. It gave her a taste of what being a human must be like. The wind made her long hair whirl as if it was playing a game. The crisp temperatures, air fresh and clean filled her with energy.

It was a Saturday morning and people were beginning their Christmas shopping. She hoped the crowds meant extra business for Clare.

The bun was gone by the time they made it to Clare's shop. Skye licked the icing off her fingers, the taste of cinnamon lingered in her mouth.

The shop wasn't open yet, but Jenny was just inside and unlocked the door for Skye.

"Good morning," Jenny said.

"Good morning," said Skye. "I'll see you two later this morning."

"Later," said Adaire.

"Good morn," said Fiachna to Jenny.

He turned and followed Adaire down the street. They were off to run a couple of errands.

Skye went inside and towards the back to put her coat in her room. The store was already warm. Bayberry candles were burning, filling the air with their lovely green scent.

A new round table sat in the middle of the display area. It was curiously empty.

The little Christmas tree was decorated and lit. More decorations hung from the ceiling and pine boughs, ivy and holly branches with bright red berries were tucked into the displays. The whole store hummed with energy.

As she passed the office, Skye noticed Clare on the floor picking things up under her desk.

"What happened?" asked Skye.

"Kittens. They're little monkeys, climbing everywhere, knocking everything off my desk," said Clare.

Skye looked in the box and saw them all there. Some nursing, others wrestling and chasing each other.

She laughed.

"It's only going to get worse you know," said Skye.

"No, it's not. I'm going to buy a cage to confine them all in at night. I can't have them tearing around the store and breaking things. And I can't have them destroying the back either. I can only baby-proof so much. There's so many electrical cords in here. I don't want anyone electrocuted. And don't get me started about breakable things."

Skye smiled and continued on to the back and unlocked her door.

She hung up her purse and coat on one of the hooks and left the door open. It would be nice to show off her room during the open house.

She put a clean sheet on the massage table, even though there were no clients today. After tidying up the room, she went to see if Clare needed help.

Clare had gotten out from under the desk and was glaring at the kittens, brushing the hair out of her face. She wore a green beaded blouse that looked like one of Emma's creations. It suited her, made her look radiant.

"Can I help with anything?" asked Skye.

"You could go hang out by the door. Kristin's coming early, and Mary, too. She's bringing the food. Help them carry their stuff in and keep everyone else out till ten." Clare glanced at her watch. "That's twenty minutes from now. I need to make some tea. I didn't get enough sleep last night."

"You're stressed," said Skye. "Take some time to breathe while you're waiting for the tea to steep."

"I will," said Clare.

"No. I'm serious. Go stand in a corner and breathe. For five minutes."

That made Clare pay attention.

"You can't be effective and make it through the day, do the things you need to do well, if you're a jangled mess," said Skye.

"Okay. I'll get the tea going and take a time out. I promise."

"Good."

Skye went to the front door and stood there.

Jenny had just finished loading up the cash register and asked, "Are you taking over the door?"

"Yes."

"Good, I've got to get some things from the back."

She went into the back room.

Marcella appeared at the door and Skye let her in.

"Sorry I'm late, couldn't find my shoes," she said, rushing towards the back while shrugging out of her coat.

A blue car pulled in front and parked. Skye recognized Mary from the Samhain ritual. Mary got out and opened the boot of her car. Skye went out and helped carry in platters of food that Mary handed to her.

She headed towards the empty table, just as Jenny came running out of the back room, carrying a large red cloth.

"Hang on," she said, swooshing the cloth in the air and unfolding it. It floated down on top of the round table and she pulled it around evening it up.

"There," Jenny said. "Now it's ready for food."

Then she disappeared into the back again.

Skye set the platters down and went out for more.

By the time she and Mary finished, the table was filled with platters of food, large dispensers of coffee, apple cider and tea. There was a table in the back that looked nearly identical.

Clare came out of the office and said, "Glorious. It looks perfect. You've outdone yourself, Mary."

"Thanks for the chance to cater your open house. It's just the break I was looking for."

"Make sure you put some of your cards by the cash register. And everyone, when people compliment the food, point them to Mary," said Clare.

Jenny nodded, she was already sampling a muffin. Marcella was sipping a cup of tea.

Clare glanced at her watch and said, "It's ten. Is everything ready?"

"Everything's perfect," said Jenny. "Open the door."

Clare unlocked the door.

Kristin was the first one in. Complete with boxes of supplies for her workshop.

Skye helped carry the boxes to the back.

"Thanks Skye. I'm gonna take a few minutes to set up and then I'll join all of you up front."

Skye went to the front of the store, past the closed office door where a lot of mewing and hissing was going on.

She poured herself some tea and added a slurp of cream.

"Skye, you have to try some of this food," said Jenny.

"I will in a bit. I'm still full from breakfast."

Four customers were in the store shopping and eating. Two of them looked vaguely familiar. Maybe they'd come to the ritual or were regulars.

The door opened and in walked a tall man with golden brown hair down to his waist. It was braided into thin strands and beaded in the manner of Fae. But there was something about him that read completely false.

Skye stared at him. He wore brown leather trousers and a leather vest over a white linen shirt, no coat, but heavy tan boots.

When he looked around and saw her, he gave her a charming smile. His golden brown eyes lit up. For a flash, not long enough for humans to catch, but for her to see, he showed her the set of antlers on his head.

So, he was Fae. An earth spirit.

He walked towards her and said, "Are you Skye?"

"Yes," she said.

"I'm Kian."

"Greetings," she said, bowing.

He bowed in return.

"I've come to protect you," he said.

More people came in the door and Skye took him into the back. They passed Clare who raised an eyebrow at her.

He didn't seem fazed by the journey here, not like Fiachna had been.

"How are things? In Faerie?"

Kian shook his head.

"Not good. I don't think we should be going to war. There aren't enough warriors to fight the Fomorians. But who am I to say?"

"You don't think Faerie stands a chance?"

"Egan's trying to teach them battle strategies. The elders are teaching the warriors more magic than is good for them. I don't know how it will all end."

Skye nodded. Warriors weren't meant to know the most powerful magic. They weren't always the most well balanced Fae. Many of them were probably too young to have that much power.

"Who are all those humans?" he motioned to the front of the shop.

"Clare owns the shop, Jenny and Marcella work here. The others are customers. And in the back is Kristin, she's setting up for a workshop she's teaching."

"Workshop?" he asked.

"It's where a group of people get together and one person teaches them. In this case, they're making things."

How could she explain making fairy houses to a Fae straight out of Faerie?

He nodded.

"Where are Fiachna and Adaire? I understood Fiachna was guarding both of you?"

"They had errands to run. They'll be here soon. I'm safe here."

"Is this the place where the Fomorian came, night after night?"

"Yes, but he's gone. He never harmed anyone here, I believe was searching for the others."

"You were lucky," he said.

"We're safe here."

'You are deluded. Fae are safe nowhere now."

"Is it that bad?" asked Skye.

"We are at war. Most of the Fomorians are not very smart, their power makes up for their stupidity. There are enough of them who are sharp-witted to cause us great harm."

Skye nodded. She didn't want to think about the war. This was a celebration, for Clare, for the other humans.

She just wanted to focus on that.

Worries about the war and Aidan kept interrupting her thoughts.

Chapter 25 ~ Clare

Clare picked an empty paper cup off a display shelf and chucked it in the bin beside the food table.

The open house was going well. Kristin was in back teaching people how to make fairy houses. Mary had brought endless amounts of food and kept the tables replenished.

Lots of customers, old and new, were shopping and Jenny and Marcella were restocking the store every chance they got. It was a good thing, she'd put all those extra orders in last month.

Clare had spent all morning walking around the store and greeting people. Chatting them up.

She'd had countless cups of tea and far too many mini buns and cakes. The sugar was making her want to curl up somewhere and take a nap.

The door opened and Raven came in, followed by Fiachna and Adaire. Who were carrying long carved posts.

"Good morning," Clare said. 'Or is it afternoon?"

"Good afternoon," said Fiachna. He had a huge grin on his face.

Adaire simply nodded. Clare had noticed she didn't talk much.

"Hi," said Raven, closing the door behind them.

"What's all this?" asked Clare.

"You'll see," said Fiachna. "It's your open house gift."

They walked into the back, weaving between display cases and clumps of people. Clare followed them, curious.

They put the four posts down near the wall closest to Skye's room and went back out the front door.

Clare went around the corner of the backstock shelving and watched Kristin for a while. It was half past noon. She was supposed to be finished at noon, but people just kept coming in.

She sidled up to her and when Kristin paused, Clare asked, "Do you want to stop?"

"I'm having fun. I'm good to keep going. Tell me when I need to get out of the way for Malcolm."

"I think he's coming at 1:30. You'll need to be cleaned up by then."

"Oh good. Another forty-five minutes then. I'll carry on. I'm having a blast."

"Good," said Clare.

She moved back towards the front, but stopped just beyond the shelves, where Fiachna and Adaire were working. Skye's new friend, Kian, was watching them intently.

They had laid out a square of posts on top of a large piece of plywood which served as a bottom, and fitted them together. There were notches where the pieces joined together. Then they inserted six upright posts that were taller than she was. Whatever they were building was large.

They added a post in the center. The posts weren't all perfectly straight and even. Some were slightly curved and bumpy, with bark still on them. As if they had come from trees recently cut down.

Clare watched mesmerized.

Raven came up to her and watched as well, while sipping coffee.

"Great coffee," she said. "Mary is so brilliant. She has such a gift for creating good food."

"I noticed, that's why I hired her. And I plan to keep hiring her for every event where we're serving food."

"That's wonderful. She's needed to get her catering business going for a long time, but she doesn't like to toot her own horn."

"What are they making?" asked Clare.

"You'll see," said Raven. "Skye called me last night and asked if I'd be willing to haul all the stuff they'd collected. So, I got my brother's truck and we loaded it up this morning. They're amazing woodworkers."

Skye got the ladder out for them and Adaire climbed up and began fitting in posts on the top of the structure.

It was going to be large. Taller and wider than Clare was tall.

Fiachna unrolled screening and began to tie it onto the wood posts with sisal rope. He wound it round and round the post until no wood could be seen.

Clare noticed quite a few customers were now standing around watching.

She should go check out front.

Raven put a hand on her arm and said, "Marcella and Jenny have got it covered. Stay. Enjoy this. It's not often you get to see Fae create things. It's amazing."

And it was. They worked incredibly fast. Just the two of them. And whatever this was, it was a work of art. Rustic and elegant all at the same time.

It almost shone with magic.

As soon as Adaire got the top posts on, she covered the top with a piece of pre-cut screen and began weaving rope around everything to secure it the screening.

Malcolm was standing on her other side.

"Do you need to set up?" she asked the large, burly bearded man.

"No. I came early for snacks," he said, holding up a piece of the coffee cake. "I love Mary's cooking. I didn't expect this. What craftsmen these two are. It's an honor to watch them."

"Amazing isn't it?" Clare said.

Fiachna had finished screening three sides and moved to the fourth. Adaire was done with the top and she put up what looked like a screen door. Pounding pegs through one side of it.

The structure looked like a small house. But why the screening? Why not wood panels?

After Adaire finished, she went inside and attached flat wood pieces to several posts. Two sets looked like stairs. And there were two wide flat crossbeams that she wove braided sisal across, making a sort of wobbly bridge or platform.

Fiachna and Adaire finished at the same time. There was no leftover wood, screening or rope.

Everyone clapped and they bowed.

Fiachna said, "It's all yours."

"Thank you, but I have no idea what it is."

"It's for the cats," said Adaire.

"The kittens," corrected Fiachna. "And the cat."

Clare clapped her hand over her mouth.

"Oh my. This is wonderful. Thank you." She hugged Adaire who smiled and Fiachna who promptly turned red with embarrassment, but kept grinning.

Adaire opened the door and Clare went in. From inside, it looked like a spacious fun place to be. Fiachna came in, bending over so as not to hit his head on the door. He pointed out the ledges for kittens to sit on and the places for them to climb. There were two larger, padded ledges for them to sleep on.

"It's perfect," she said.

She went outside and walked around it and other people went inside and looked around. Touching the structure with wonder lighting up their faces.

Kian said, after everyone had a chance to go inside, "Don't you think it's time to put the kittens inside?"

Clare, Skye and Adaire got the food, water and litter box and set them in opposite corners. Then a clean blanket in a new cardboard box for the cat bed. Fiachna carried the kittens to the new space.

Clare watched as Kian gently picked up Pirate and carried her to the back room. Even though she was quite capable of walking. It looked as if he was glowing as he petted the cat.

Was he a healer too?

She'd known he was Fae when he walked in the door. He had that same tall elegance about him that they all did. Even Meredith, the older stooped and rather lumpy Fae, had looked elegant somehow.

Clare stood outside the enclosure watching the kittens. They were exploring the floor. Some of them took the opportunity to eat the wet food. Pirate walked around the kittens, sniffing at the enclosure and then climbed up one set of stairs and sat on a perch grooming herself.

She clearly approved of the new space.

There was quite an audience by that time.

Clare said, "I don't know what to say. Thank you so much, all of you."

Adaire said, "It was Fiachna's idea. To create a space where they can play and not get into trouble."

"Thank you," said Clare, touching his arm.

"You are very welcome," he said, beaming and bowing to her slightly.

Pirate finished her bath and lay down, hanging over the ledge and watching the kittens below. They were chasing each other around the center post, trying to climb up the uprights and wrestling.

They couldn't quite make it up past the first level. Their muscles weren't strong enough yet, but they were growing so fast, she figured by next week they'd be up at the top level.

"They are so adorable," said Kristin.

Clare glanced at her watch, then walked around the shelving to the back corner. Kristin was just taking the last of her supplies out with the help of a woman who'd been building fairy houses.

Malcolm was beginning to set up. Clare helped him put paint sets and brushes around the table. Along with paper towels along and cups of water. The people who had signed up to paint drums began to appear. Over half had bought new drums today and the rest brought drums from home.

Malcolm began his lecture by showing them the painted drums he'd brought and pointing them to the front of the store to look at the painted ones for sale, after he'd finished a quick lecture.

Clare went back towards the front and saw Adaire and Kian sitting on the floor, watching the kittens play. Pirate was asleep on a perch.

The front was filled with customers. Mary was keeping the tables stocked and had just put out a platter of mini quiches. Clare grabbed two, relieved to find something that wasn't sweet. Then she noticed the platter of cold cuts and cheeses. She'd have to come back for those.

Jenny was at the cash register and Marcella was working the floor. Clare joined her, asking people if they were finding what they were looking for.

After a time Marcella and Jenny switched. A redheaded woman came in who Jenny immediately hugged. She pulled her friend into the back. A couple of minutes later Jenny came back out front.

"That was my friend Amanda. The one who's elderly cat died a couple of months ago. Do you know which kittens will be available for adoption?"

"The solid gray, the gray tabby and the tortoiseshell. The grays need to be indoor/outdoor and the tortoiseshell needs to be an only cat."

"How do you know that?"

"Skye."

"Well then. Good to know. I'll go tell Amanda."

Clare continued to chat with customers. After a time, she went to the back and checked on Malcolm. He was walking around the table, talking to people painting their drums.

Kian and Amanda were in with the kittens. She was holding the tortoiseshell, who was cuddled up around the woman's neck, looking very happy.

Skye and Adaire and several other people were in Skye's room talking. Skye seemed to be giving them a tour, talking about the art work on her walls.

Clare turned around to see Fiachna standing there, watching Kian.

"I don't know how to thank you for this. It's absolutely perfect."

He laughed. "You have already thanked me three times. That is enough, I think."

"I was just so surprised. I only voiced it last night that I needed a cage for the kittens, only just realized it," she said.

"I have been watching them, growing and getting stronger and wilder. They needed to leave your office and have a place to play without destroying things. You have so many beautiful, fragile things in the shop and back here on the shelves. It seemed the best solution until they are old enough to be out in the rest of the store."

"By that time, some of them will be adopted."

"Well, for the cats who stay here, they will have a comfortable place to retreat to. You can hang fabric over the cage and give them a dark, quiet place to go to when there is too much going on," he said.

"You've given this a lot of thought."

"I have a great deal of time to think. I am guarding two other Fae. It involves a lot of standing around. I am used to being more active, moving around the countryside. I need something to think about."

"What did you spending your time doing?" she asked.

"I used to guard the boundaries of Faerie. Walking the lines, making sure they were anchored. Fixing them if the spells had been loosened. Guarding the barrows that were anchoring points."

"So, you were always on the move?"

"Yes. Never staying in one place for long. But that made the whole countryside my home."

"I live in the first home I've ever really had, plus the shop. So I guess I have two homes."

"This feels like a home," said Fiachna. "I like being here with all the beautiful stones and the art."

"So, what type of Fae are you? You don't seem like Aidan was, or Meredith or Dylan. I don't think you're an air spirit like Skye. You seem sort of like Adaire, but completely different."

He laughed.

"I am an earth spirit, but Adaire is connected to trees. My kin are rocks. I am one of the stone people. Just like Kian belongs to the animals."

She followed his gaze to Kian who had a gray kitten on each shoulder and the orange one climbing his leg.

"So that's why you notice all the crystals and stones in the store."

"We resonate on the same level. Rocks speak to me, just as they do to some humans."

"I'm not one of them. Sometimes I wish I could hear."

"That is not your gift."

"I have a gift?" she asked, almost laughing.

"Your voice is strong, you cannot hear the quiet voices of stones or plants or the wind. Your voice is strong so you can lead. This chaotic human world needs strong, calm and reasoned voices like yours."

She'd never thought of herself as any of those things. Never wanted to be a leader. Yet she often looked up from her own life and found herself in just that position.

"It's hard to lead when I don't know where I'm going."

"The destination is less important than you might imagine, and you do not have control of that. You may have one in mind, but the world will always have other plans. It is most important to enjoy the journey."

"And where is your journey going to take you?" she asked.

"I do not know. I thought I would always be a boundary keeper. It was a life I loved, but when the boundaries were opened, well, I really do not know what the future holds for me. It has been blown wide open with this war. I hope to stay away from it. I hope it ends before it really begins. But if I am called, then I must go. The stone people are warriors."

She touched his arm. "I hope you get to stay away from it. I don't think war really ever solves anything. World War I was supposed to be the war to end all wars. Look how that turned out."

"I do not know," said Fiachna.

"It was followed by World War II, with massive destruction and an abominable number of deaths. Even after all that, humans still identify a group of other humans, label them as other and attempt to destroy them, it is happening today. War is a temporary solution. I believe we must learn to accept and live with the differences of others."

"Ah, but to get all those different voices to agree on such a thing is impossible. There will always be one group who believes that annihilation of those unlike itself is the best path."

"I don't think it has to be that way. I really do think we can all respect each other and get along."

"You are an optimist, I think. An idealist. That is a difficult road to travel in this world," he said.

"It's the only way I know how to be. It makes my life worthwhile."

"And that is why everyone likes you. You strive for things to be better."

"Is that a bad thing?" she asked.

"No. Not at all. The world needs optimists and idealists. It needs the sun, so things can grow. So life can exist. You are essential to this time and place."

"What will happen if Fae lose this war?"

"It is possible the Fomorians would destroy the human world. And then return to their slumber. Or perhaps they will simply go back to sleep after destroying the Fae. I do not pretend to understand the Fomorians. They do not always act together. They have always been a group of unruly, rebellious individuals, loosely controlled by their leader. Unpredictable."

He put her arm in his and said, "But enough of this talk. This is a celebration for your work. We should go enjoy it, not speak of a war which may not come here."

She nodded and allowed herself to be led back out front.

The table was still filled with food, although a couple of platters seemed to have disappeared. Mary had been taking things out to her car as things got used up. She had stored food waiting to come out in a cooler in her car.

There were less people wandering around the store, but a fair sized crowd. There was still the drum painting workshop going on, with lots of spectators.

Jenny came up to her and said, "We've sold out of a lot of the jewelry."

"And you restocked."

Jenny nodded. "Now all our back stock is gone."

"Guess I'll be ordering tomorrow," said Clare.

"At least you can leave the office door open now," said Jenny. "The cat corral is so amazing."

"Cat corral. I like that. Did your friend decide if she wants a kitten?"

"Yes. I forgot to tell you. She really, really wants the tortoiseshell."

"Another one down. Two left to go."

Jenny held her finger up to her forehead and said, "I predict they'll both find homes today. If they haven't already. I've heard lots of people talk about wanting a kitten. The cat corral is a great display tool."

Clare watched Fiachna talking to Kirstin. He had such an easy way about him. She loved to watch him, the way he smiled and spoke with his strong hands. He always listened with such intensity.

What would it be like to have him as a lover?

Not that she had any experience in that department to compare to. She'd never allowed anyone to get that close to her. There hadn't been many interested in the first place.

Clare shook her head and went into the back to see what was happening. Kian was in the corral with a man who she recognized from the ritual. Daniel. That was his name. They were playing with kittens.

In the far back a few people were still painting. Others were taking photographs of finished drums. Another group of people were chatting with Mary around the food table. Marcella was picking up cups of used paint water and brushes to take them into the loo to clean.

Clare felt pleased everything was going so well. She hoped everyone was getting what they needed from the day.

She felt full and contented.

There had been a lot of sales. It was a great start to the holiday shopping season. And she'd replenished the stack of flyers by the cash register at least twice. Hopefully, people would show up for the events in the next three months and get into the habit of visiting the store.

Many of the people who came for the open house were ones she'd never seen before. New potential customers. Which was encouraging.

Everyone she'd talked to about the Kristin's workshop had a wonderful time. And it looked like Malcolm's was a success as well.

Clare heard a lot of noise coming from the front and went back out.

Everyone was looking through the front window and pointing. The door was being held open, Kian brushed past her and went straight for the door. She followed him outside.

In the middle of the street stood a large herd of frightened-looking deer. They were surrounding stopped cars. Kian walked up to them, holding his arms out. They gathered towards him.

He put his face right up to a big buck's nose. She could see his lips moving, but couldn't hear what he said.

When he'd finished speaking, the tall Fae straightened up again and backed away. The deer turned and went back down the street as if they owned it. Motorists screeched to a halt, trying to avoid them.

Kian came back and stood by her, watching them.

"What did you say?"

"I told them to leave the city. To go back to the fields where they're safe. That I'd come see them tonight, up on the Tor."

"They came to see you?" she asked.

"Yes. They have things they'd like to say."

"Do they know you?"

"My kind have always been there for them."

Clare sighed.

"What I don't know about the world would fill all of London."

"Most humans left the natural world a very long time ago. Fae never have. We couldn't," he said, shrugging his shoulders.

Clare went back inside and Kian followed her.

The day waned and the crowd thinned out. Mary had been packing her things up all day as the food disappeared. It took very little to help her clean up.

Clare fed the kittens and Pirate again. Got them fresh water and emptied the cat box for the second time. The kittens were eating wet food now, as well as nursing.

She petted and hugged each of them, including Pirate, who'd come down from her perch.

"Enjoy your first night in your new home, kids," she said, closing and latching the door behind her.

Jenny had cleaned out the cash register and put everything in the bank bag. Marcella was turning lights out and doing the other closing tasks. Clare shut down the office and turned the heat in the front room down, but left it on in the back for the cats.

Skye had shut her office and she, Adaire and Kian had already left. Fiachna was standing by the door, waiting.

"Why are you still here?" she asked.

"Skye said I should be sure to walk you to the bank. She is worried about you with all the money."

"Aren't she and Adaire in more danger than I am?"

"Who is to say? I am happy to walk you to the bank," he said.

Jenny and Marcella got their coats and headed towards the door.

"Thank you so much, you two."

"Today was such fun," said Jenny. "But I'm beat. Good thing Mary left food for us. I won't have to cook tonight." She held up a paper bag.

"Don't forget your goody bag," said Marcella.

"Oh, I almost did," said Clare. She slipped her coat on, turned the back lights off, set the alarm, grabbed all her bags, closed and locked the door behind everyone.

The bank was only a block away, but it was dark. It was a Saturday night and there were still a lot of people downtown, on their way to supper or going out for the night.

Fiachna was such a tall, solid presence beside her.

She was exhausted too and didn't feel like talking. Sometimes working at the store, being so social all day took all her conversation away. Today was one of those days.

But she didn't feel awkward with him. Like she needed to fill the space with idle talk. Silence felt comfortable.

She slid the bag into the after hours deposit slot at the bank.

Then turned towards her house.

Fiachna followed her.

"You can go home if you want to. The money's safe at the bank."

"Do you want me to leave?" he asked.

"No."

"Well, then if it is all the same to you, I will walk you home safely."

"Thank you."

They walked the few blocks to her house in the silent, sleeting darkness.

Chapter 26 ~ Skye

Skye ran up the steps towards the Tor. Her human body breathless and legs rubbery. She was in a hurry to get to the top.

The cold wind whipped around her.

The others, Fiachna, Adaire and Kian, were taking the long way up, the path that wound around the mound several times. Skye wanted to spend more time at the top, where the wind would hit her at full blast.

The sun was shrouded by heavy cloud cover this morning. It was a frigid December morning, Yule. There were no humans around at the moment. They were busy getting ready for Christmas Eve and Christmas Day, or perhaps their own Yule celebrations.

Cattle and sheep grazed the luscious grass that covered the hill. Far down below, Skye saw a large herd of deer following the other Fae.

Drawn by Kian, two badgers also trailed along as well as several foxes. Even a pair of hares skittered behind the Fae.

Skye had to stop running before she reached the top. She'd let this body get too out of shape. Not enough exercise.

She breathed heavily, feeling the cold air rush inside her body. The coldness made her lungs ache.

Winter was here.

Finally, she stood on the top. The wind lifted her short, open coat, beneath which lay a thick wool jumper. To keep warm, she'd also worn corduroy trousers, wool socks and leather boots.

Skye lifted her arms and spun in circles, laughing, playing with the wind.

The only thing that would make it better would be flying, but she couldn't risk it these days.

Eventually, the others made it to the top. Far less winded. Adaire was more active than Skye had been. Fiachna and Kian were in their own bodies, not human ones.

"I just love it up here," said Skye.

"Yes, you've told us, half a million times," said Adaire.

"Well, it's as close as I can get to flying. Look at the wonderful view, the countryside laid below us, almost like a map. It's comforting being able to see so far again. It makes me feel clear."

Fiachna laid his hand on her arm. A gesture that said he understood what she was going through and how imprisoned she felt not being able to fly.

Adaire nodded.

Kian said, "It is beautiful."

He patted one of the nearby black and white cows between the ears. The cows and sheep had stopped grazing when he arrived and joined the deer and other animals.

Kian always seemed to collect an entourage.

A flock of birds swirled away from the Tor. They became a dark cloud, squishing together, then flowing apart. The cloud changed shape again and again until it disappeared as the birds landed back on the stonework of the Tor.

"When are you going to tell her, Fiachna?" asked Adaire.

That caught Skye's attention.

"Tell who, what?" she asked.

Fiachna just shrugged.

"Tell Clare that he loves her and that he's been called," said Adaire.

"Called?" asked Skye, feeling slightly panicked.

"Egan called me this morning, and Adaire as well. We must return to Faerie."

"When?" asked Skye, panicked. "And why Adaire? She's not a warrior."

It felt as if a dark fist clutched at her heart. She didn't want to lose her friends, or to be called. To have to return to Faerie. To war.

"We leave in two days," said Fiachna. "The day after Clare's Christmas gathering."

"I was called to help heal the trees. They're suffering from the war," said Adaire.

Skye's heart sank. Even an air spirit like her could recognize that the trees of Faerie were like none other on Earth. But she would miss her two friends terribly.

"Are you going to tell Clare?" asked Skye.

"Adaire says I should. I want to. But is it fair to her? To a human? Their lives are so short. I do not know when I will be able to return. This war could last a season or millennia."

"Yes, you should tell her. Otherwise you're not giving her any choice in the matter. She can then decide whether to wait for you or not. You can't just leave without telling her that you love her. That's not fair."

"I agree," said Kian. "I don't understand humans very well, but every creature alive deserves love and to know they're loved by others. She has a big heart, which she keeps very protected. If she doesn't get a chance to open her heart she will live a very unfulfilled life. Give her a chance."

Fiachna sighed deeply. "Then I will tell her. Tomorrow. On Christmas."

They were silent after that. Taking in the world around them.

The smell of the fresh air. The connectedness of everything. The steam coming off the sheep, cows and deer. The mist falling all around them. The sharp flapping of the birds' wings and the grunting of the deer.

Skye's hair dampened from the moisture. She breathed deeply and licked her lips. She wanted this war to end and for there never again be war.

Skye wished she had the power to make it happen.

She formed her thoughts into a solid request and spoke it to her gloved fingertips, then blew the desire out to the wind. She imagined it spreading her wish like the cloud of birds fanned out. Giving the wish to other winds until her desire travelled everywhere. Taking root in fertile places. Lodging in every single beating heart. Every cell of each living creature from amoebas to gods.

Could it come true?

Her wish for peace?

She had to believe it was possible in order to do her work. Her healing abilities depended on balance. There was never any balance with war.

Chapter 27 ~ Clare

Clare scurried across her small kitchen, cursing at the pot boiling over. She turned the heat down, picking the pot up and waited for it to cool a bit before she put it back down on the burner again.

What had she been thinking? She never cooked.

Clare set a timer and opened the oven to check the turkey. It was coming along nicely. Nearly done. The smell made her mouth water. Closing the door, she went back to the sink to finish washing up the cooking dishes with hot, soapy water.

She splashed water on her gray T-shirt, yoga pants and the green tiled floor. She wiped up the stone tiles with a paper towel and tossed it in the bin.

Clare had never hosted a Christmas dinner before. She'd always avoided the holiday as an adult, having participated in so many awful ones as a child.

But this year, she had a family.

Finally.

She'd invited Marcella, Raven, Kristin, Skye, Fiachna, Adaire, Kian and Emma. She'd invited all the unattached people who had no one to spend the day with.

She invited Jenny, even though she knew Jenny was spending it with her parents and her two sons. Of course, Jenny had said thanks, but no.

Clare had a full house coming. At least she'd thought ahead and told everyone it was potluck, assigning them a category of food to bring, so she wouldn't have to cook everything herself. She'd volunteered for turkey, stuffing, potatoes and gravy. The rest would be provided by others.

She looked around. The kitchen didn't look too bad, considering. She glanced at the clock. She still had a bit of time to tidy up the piles of clean dishes and put away unused ingredients. The place sort of looked like a mad engineer's workshop.

There was a dull crashing sound from her bedroom. She went down the hall and opened the door, sliding in and closing it before anyone could escape.

Pirate was sitting up, on the green down comforter on the bed, looking sleepy eyed.

"Hello, is everyone okay?" Clare asked.

A mew came from under the bed and Honey came out. The orange kitten looked suspiciously at the lumpy pile of books on the floor. They'd been on her bedside table. He was followed by Blackheart and Shadow.

Clare picked up the books and set them up on her dresser. Hopefully out of reach.

She squatted down and petted the kittens.

"Are you kids all right?"

She picked them up one by one and set them on the cat tower by the window.

"Here's a good place for you to play. I promise I'll spend time with you as soon as I get dinner under control. You'll get to come to the party. Promise."

Faerie Contact

She'd brought them all home for the holidays.

Clare had decided to close the shop for a week, through New Year's. A week off with paid vacation for her staff. They'd had such a spectacular season, sales wise that she could afford it. She really hated stores who made their staff work on holidays.

She hadn't wanted the kittens to be alone in the store for that long. They were all weaned and eating solid food well.

Jenny's friend had happily taken the tortoiseshell home for her Christmas present and Malcolm had ended up adopting the solid gray kitten and the gray tabby. He lived on a farm and they'd get to go outside and hunt during the day and keep him company inside in the evening.

So, she'd brought everyone home with her last night and they were currently locked in her bedroom since Clare couldn't supervise them while cooking.

She left the bedroom, checked on the potatoes, which were boiling along nicely. Two more minutes and she'd pull them and put them in the pan to roast. At least she'd done that before. The whole turkey thing was new for her and quite daunting.

Clare walked into the dining room. She'd set the table much earlier. It looked beautiful. She'd found fresh holly with berries and a few small yew branches on her walk yesterday for a bouquet.

The living room looked good. When she moved in she'd painted the walls a warm terra cotta color and it looked beautiful with the golden brown wood floor. She still loved it. The dark brown furniture made it feel warm and cozy. A few books lay on the coffee table, but there was still plenty of room for glasses.

The timer buzzed and she turned off the burner, scooping the potatoes out with a slotted spoon. Once they were all in the roasting pan, she drizzled olive oil over them, sprinkled salt and pepper and fresh, pungent rosemary from a bush in her back garden. She stirred the potatoes, rolling them over till they were coated with oil and slid the pan into the oven, on the lower rack, beneath the turkey and stuffing rack.

She pulled the stuffing out to check it. It was nicely browned, so she put it on top of the stove, covering it with a piece of foil to keep warm. Then set the timer to remind herself to turn the potatoes so they'd brown evenly.

About twenty more minutes for the turkey and guests would be coming about then. Time to pull herself together.

She went back into the bedroom to change. The kittens were all sleeping on the cat tower, which had two beds on it. Honey was on one by himself. Blackheart and Shadow were all rolled up into one big ball. Clare had named the black kitten Shadow, because she always followed Blackheart, the white kitten with the black tail tip and black heart under her chin.

Clare chose the long sleeved blouse she'd worn at the open house, made by Emma. It was beaded and a lovely green shade. It made her feel elegant. She also slipped into some black trousers and black flats. Without socks. She felt too warm from all the cooking.

She brushed her hair, deciding against jewelry. The beaded top was enough. Slipping out of the bedroom, she went into the living room and turned on some new agey music. Soft Celtic style fiddle started up.

Clare lit candles in the living room and dining room.

The timer went off and she stirred the potatoes, turning the chunks over to brown all sides.

Then the door bell rang. Her guest were here.

Emma and Kristin were the first. Marcella, as always, the last to arrive. People brought their food into the kitchen and Clare arranged it on the kitchen island, uncovering the dishes and finding servings spoons.

When everyone was there, Clare opened the bedroom door so the cats could come out and entertain the guests. She busied herself in the kitchen taking the finished potatoes out and putting them on a serving platter. She'd set up the island as a serving area. The dining room table was full enough with everyone's plates, silverware and glasses.

The turkey was finished and she pulled it out of the oven while people mingled and chatted and poured wine that the Fae had brought.

She got the turkey onto a platter and left it to relax a bit before slicing it, like the recipe had said to do.

Fiachna came into the kitchen.

"Is this a good time to talk to you?" he asked.

"Sure. I've got a few minutes before I need to do this," she pointed at the turkey.

"I have hesitated to say anything before this, but I am out of time. Egan has called Adaire and I back to Faerie. We must leave tomorrow."

Clare closed her eyes. A wave of blackness threatened to take her down.

He touched her arm and she met his eyes. Warmth spread through her entire body as if the sun shone on her from his touch.

He said, "I love you. I have not felt this way in thousands of years. But I knew it the first time I met you. I just have not been able to find the words."

"What does that mean to you?" she asked. "I won't pretend to understand Fae."

"It means I want to spend every moment with you. Even though I must leave tomorrow. My heart will be here with you. No matter what else happens. I will return as soon as I am able."

"I suppose you know how I feel about you."

"I do not," he said.

She took a deep breath and blurted it out, before she lost her nerve. "I love you too. Even though I don't really know you. Don't know how we could have a life together. Like I said, I don't fully understand who Fae are."

"We are all different. You and I could have a life together. A very good life. Filled with love and laughter."

She nodded, her eyes welling up with emotion.

He took her hand and turned the palm side up. Then he set a ring on it. Two strands of a pinkish yellow metal wove around each other.

"This is beautiful," she said.

"I made it for you. It's gold and copper melted together and then two pieces twined together. I wear its twin," he said, holding up his hand. "I will understand if you do not want to wear it. It is a promise made facing an uncertain future. I give it to you all the same. Hoping that if not now, then sometime, you will decide to wear it."

Clare didn't know what to say.

She loved him, but how could she commit to what he was asking? What if he never came back? What if he was killed in the war?

"I don't know if I can keep this," she said. It was incredibly beautiful and precious, made even more so, knowing that he made it.

"You must. No one else can wear it. I understand your hesitation. You think you might never see me again. That is a possibility. Put the ring away and when you are ready, it will be there. I will come back to you."

"I'll wear it on my right hand," she said, putting it on. "Until you return."

He stroked her hair with his fingers. She closed her eyes in delight.

Then he kissed her and she felt a surge of energy move throughout her entire body, illuminating all the darkness that lingered inside her.

She returned his kiss.

"Hey," said Kristin. "Can I help with anything in here? Oops, guess not. Never mind. I was never here."

She disappeared back into the dining room.

Clare laughed.

"I better get dinner served."

She got a knife out and began slicing the turkey.

"Can I help?"

"You can take the potatoes out of the oven and set them there," she pointed to an empty space.

She glanced up and noticed he carried the pan with bare hands.

"You'll burn yourself," she said, panicking.

"I am stone Fae. We don't burn," he said, closing the oven door.

She really didn't have a clue about Fae.

"I don't know how to carve turkeys," she said. "I've never made one before."

"No one will care what it looks like," Fiachna said. "It smells delicious. My mouth is watering."

When she'd finished carving the turkey, Clare went into the dining room and said, "All the food's ready to eat. Grab a plate and dish up in the kitchen. I'd like to wait till everyone's seated before we begin eating."

It didn't take long for everyone to dish up and return to the table. In the meantime, she rounded up the kittens and Pirate and put them back in the bedroom.

"I'll save all of you leftover turkey. You can come back when we're done eating."

When everyone was sitting, Clare made sure the glasses were filled.

"I'd like to make a toast," she looked around the table, making sure everyone heard. "When I came here six months ago, I had no idea all that would happen. I hoped I'd open the store and that it would provide me with enough income to live. I had no idea I'd make so many dear friends who'd become my family. Or meet so many interesting people, not all of them human."

Everyone laughed.

"I'd like to toast to friendship. Friends who've become family. You mean the world to me."

"To friends and family," everyone said, then drank.

Fiachna was sitting on one side of her, Emma on the other.

She felt Fiachna's thigh against hers, he made her feel doubly warm and contented.

The table was a bit small for nine people. Everyone was scrunched in close, but it worked out.

After they'd been eating for a while, Fiachna said, in a loud voice, "I do not know if humans make announcements during meals, but Fae do. I have something to say."

Everyone stopped talking.

"You all know there is a war going on between Faerie and the Fomorians. Aidan, Dylan and Meredith, who you may have met at Samhain, are fighting, each in their own ways. Adaire and I have been called back to Faerie. Adaire to heal trees and I to join in the battle. Kian and Skye will be staying here for the time being."

Clare looked around the table. The only ones who didn't look shocked were the other Fae.

Fiachna continued, "I have very much enjoyed my time here with all of you. In all my years I have only watched humans from afar. To walk among you and be treated as one of you has indeed been an honor. I am looking forward to the end of this war and to returning here."

He took Clare's hand, beneath the table and a surge of warmth came from him, passing through her.

Raven asked, "When do you think the war will end?"

Adaire said, "There's no way to tell. From what I understand, we're at a standstill. The Fomorians are much more powerful. But the Fae are infinitely more numerous and we're strategists. The Fomorians blunder through on strength and power."

Fiachna said, "It could end tomorrow or …"

"Never," said Kian, stirring his roasted potatoes in a pool of gravy.

Skye said, "I hope it ends soon. And diplomatically. I think an agreement that is eternal would be best."

"The Fomorians would never agree to such a thing. They're too short sighted," said Kian.

"War is always painful," said Skye.

"I am sorry I had to bring the war up," said Fiachna. "I wanted to explain Adaire's and my own disappearance. Come, this is a celebration. Let us enjoy this time and be thankful for the day."

He raised his glass and everyone clinked glasses again.

Clare sipped the lovely burgundy. The flavors swirled around in her mouth, changing by the second. Even the aftertaste was different than the first.

Emma, who sat next to her, asked, "What color blouse shall I make you for Imbolc?"

Clare said, "I haven't thought that far. The colors of wall fabric will be white, blue and yellow."

"Blue then, with white and gold beading," said Emma. "It'll look brilliant on you."

Emma's face looked far away as if she was planning out the design of the blouse in detail.

Everyone finished their main course, took their dishes into the kitchen and got dessert plates. There were four desserts: apple pie, Christmas pudding, a chocolate yule log and trifle.

Clare had to try them all.

The pie had a flaky buttery crust, the filling was a melange of apples, cinnamon, cloves, raisins and nutmeg. It was a feast. By the time she made it through the slivers of the other desserts, Clare felt like she would burst.

She leaned back and listened to the conversations.

And thought about Fiachna.

She decided to ask him to spend the night. Did Fae do that? She had no idea what they thought about casual sex, although it wasn't casual for her. She'd never had sex with anyone besides herself.

But it was time and he was who she wanted.

No matter what happened next.

As people sat, sipped tea and ate dessert, Clare felt movement. She wondered if she'd drunk too much wine. But everyone else at the table looked as alarmed as she felt.

"Earthquake," yelled Skye. "Get under the table."

Clare scootched out of her chair and crawled under the table. They were all facing each other.

It would be laughable if the earth wasn't shaking.

She worried about the cats. And her shop. The building was old.

The shaking stopped

Skye said, "Wait. There might be aftershocks. Just sit down and hang out for a few minutes."

Clare sat down and looked at Fiachna. His eyes were closed and his face relaxed. As if he wasn't really there.

Everyone was quietly listing the places, animals and people they hoped were all right.

The Fae were all silent. Kian had a far away look in his eyes and Adaire's eyes were closed as well. Skye was the only Fae who was truly present.

All the humans looked as afraid as Clare felt.

Skye said, "I've been through a few earthquakes. In L.A. and Seattle."

She was scrolling through her mobile. Looking for news Clare assumed.

"Here we go," she said. "It was a big one. 6.7. Off the west coast. Lots of damage in Penzance and Hayle. Tsunamis expected. I'm sure glad we're inland."

There was another tremor and Clare cringed inside, imagining things falling and breaking in the shop. She had insurance, but any art was irreplaceable.

What would she do if the building was badly damaged? She'd have to begin all over again.

Fiachna opened his eyes after the tremor and said, "It is over. He has passed by."

His face looked wrinkled with worry.

"He?" asked Skye.

"It was a Fomorian. Passing through. And angry."

"Out in the sea?" asked Skye.

Fiachna said, "Yes."

Faerie Contact

Clare asked, "Can we get out from under the table?"

"Yes," said Fiachna.

She crawled out from underneath and ran down the hall to check on the kittens and Pirate. They were all still sleeping, but looked up when she opened the door.

"Okay, well, you guys are calm. That's good. I'll be back in a bit."

She walked through the house, checking on things. A few things were knocked over, but there was no damage done. She hoped the same was true at the shop.

People were picking up their dishes and taking them into the kitchen. Kristin had pushed up her sleeves and was beginning to clean off dishes and load them into the empty dishwasher.

"You don't have to do that," said Clare.

Raven, who was putting food into Clare's plastic containers, said, "You probably need to go check on the shop. We'll clean up here."

"Really?" asked Clare.

"Yes, really, now go," said Kristin.

"I'll help here too," said Marcella.

"Could you put a few pieces of turkey in the cats' food bowls? I promised them treats. As long as someone's here supervising them, they can be out," said Clare.

"Okay," said Marcella. "I'll hang out till you get back."

"Are you sure?"

"Yeah, I'd rather avoid the chaos and drama that my housemates are probably doing right now."

"You really need to find a new place to live," said Clare.

"I have a place," said Raven. "A flat I rent out. What are you looking for?"

Clare didn't stick around to listen. She went to the coat closet and pulled out her coat. Then picked up her purse.

"Thank you, all of you for coming. It was a wonderful Christmas celebration for me," Clare said.

The Fae were gathered in one corner talking.

Fiachna waved goodbye to them and turned to follow Clare.

"We will talk later," he said to them. "I need to go with Clare."

That surprised her. She hadn't assumed anyone would go with her.

They quickly walked the several blocks to the shop. People were outside their homes, checking around their yards, probably looking for damage.

The weather was nippy, but dry at least.

Fiachna took her gloved hand half way there and a surge of warmth and well-being flowed through her.

She would miss his presence so much. A wave of darkness came from the depths of her soul, its presence pressing down on her. Extinguishing the brightness in her life.

"Do not regret what has not happened," he said. "Be present with me now. Enjoy this short time we have together."

She nodded, understanding what he meant. It was much more difficult to do.

High Street was abuzz with people. This wasn't an ordinary holiday. Not with the earthquake. People were out walking. Gathering together for support.

Only one of the buildings looked badly damaged. The windows broken, shattered on the sidewalk. The wood around the windows cracked, as was the brickwork above them.

Clare looked at the outside of her shop. Everything seemed to be as she left it. Except the alarm was going off.

She unlocked the door and walked quickly to the back, sidestepping powdery debris on the floor. Clare punched in the numbers and the alarm stopped blaring. One day she'd get a silent alarm.

She switched lights on, relieved that the power was still on.

Fiachna had followed her in and closed the door. He was bent over picking up a couple of large stones which hadn't been in the case. The beautiful purple amethyst cluster had shattered. Still, he gathered the pieces in his large hand.

When he had finished, Clare watched as he held his other hand over the top, enclosing the amethyst pieces between them. Fiachna closed his eyes and when he removed his top hand, the stone was whole again.

Clare gasped.

"You can heal stones."

"I am a stone spirit," he said, gently setting the crystal down on the counter.

Of course.

Clare looked around at the ceiling and walls. No cracks in front, but there was a lot of dislodged dust, or maybe stuff from the ceiling shifting. She wasn't sure.

She picked up and re shelved books, so she could walk through the store. The quake had knocked over one entire shelf. Jewelry displays had fallen to the floor and she put a tangle of pendants on the glass counter to deal with when the shop opened again.

Fiachna continued to heal any broken stones and even fixed a cracked glass shelf in the crystal display case.

Clare went into the back, opening the office. Everything looked fine in there. In the far back, huge chunks of plaster had fallen, revealing the woodwork above it. One piece had dropped, just above the cat corral. But it had hit the floor off to the side as if repelled by the structure. The cat corral area was completely clear of any debris.

The floor elsewhere was covered in white dust or chunks of plaster.

Fiachna came up behind her.

"Well, at least the cat corral isn't damaged," she said, laughing.

"It was made to repel attacks on it, just in case. I thought the attacks would come from the inside though," he smiled.

Clare looked inside Skye's room. It seemed intact. Nothing even knocked over.

All in all, she'd been very lucky.

Clare set the alarm again and they left the shop. She'd clean up another day.

Maybe come in early to vacuum on the day the shop opened again. She didn't think there'd be a rush of customers. It would be a weekday and January would probably be quite slow. Except for days or nights when she was having events.

They walked back to her house. It was dark outside and growing colder.

She shivered in her heavy wool coat.

Fiachna put his arm around her and she felt warm again.

She sighed, trying to work up her nerve. It was now or never.

"Would you spend the night with me?" she asked. "I don't know how you Fae feel about sex and I don't want to insult you."

He looked at her, his eyebrows raised. "How could I be insulted? We Fae are less rigid about sex than humans, I have heard. We cannot conceive children unless both of us are willing. It is a conscious act. We do not have diseases. But still, this is very important to me. I am honored by your request. Yes, I will spend the night. Although, I will have to leave very, very early in the morning."

She nodded.

Back at the house, Clare found no one had left and the place was immaculate.

Kian and Marcella were playing with the kittens, watching them attack curling ribbon from gifts people had brought earlier, insisting that she open them immediately after they arrived.

Skye and Adaire sat talking. Kristin was wiping out splatters in Clare's oven. Raven was organizing all the leftover food in the refrigerator. Emma was wiping down the counters.

"Oh my goodness," said Clare. "My kitchen hasn't been this clean since I moved in."

"How's the shop?" asked Raven.

"In pretty good shape. Except the back room. Lots of plaster on the floor. I'm pretty sure it'll all need to be redone. Lots of things fell off shelves, but the shop's mostly fine."

"That's great to hear, well not about the back room, but it could have been worse," said Emma.

"Why haven't you gone to your shop?" asked Clare.

"The landlord called. He was outside of it and I gave him permission to go in and check. I really didn't want to. He called back and said everything looked good. Some of my plastic dye bottles were tipped over, but he righted them. There wasn't spillage. So everything's fine. I was lucky."

"Well, I'm off," said Raven. "Gotta go check on my house."

The others left at the same time.

Clare said goodbye to Adaire. Would she ever see her again?

Fiachna told the other Fae, "I will see you early in the morning. When it is time to leave."

When everyone was gone, Clare felt awkward around Fiachna.

But he took her in his arms and kissed her deeply on the lips. It felt as if she'd always been with him. Like they already knew each other intimately.

The night was glorious.

The morning heartbreaking.

Chapter 28 ⚜ Skye

Skye stood in the kitchen of the cottage. It felt cold and she shivered even in her warm blue jumper and jeans. Watching Adaire drink green juice and ready herself for the trek back to Faerie. Fiachna hadn't arrived yet.

She hadn't slept last night. Just put her human body to bed. She and Adaire had stayed up all night talking. Who knew when they'd see each other again?

Skye wrapped her long fingers around the mug of mint tea. More for comfort than anything.

The house was eerily silent.

Filled with unspoken fears and events.

Kian was walking around outside in the darkness before dawn. Whispering to hedgehogs and field mice.

"I'm really looking forward to going back to Faerie," said Adaire. "Of being useful. Helping the trees."

"I know. You've helped the trees around here though, and the garden is lovely. I'll miss you though."

Adaire nodded. "I'll miss you too, but we'll see each other again. This war will end. You'll be able to fly again. Faerie will be healed and I'll walk the Earth again, healing other forests."

Skye sipped the mint tea, sensing the flavors unfold in her mouth.

Adaire said, "I have heard tell of a special garden in Faerie. In that garden is a white flower that blooms for one night every hundred years. It is said that to smell that blossom will send one into such complete rapture that they will never again feel pain at the world's problems. I will seek out that garden. Find some of the nectar for the healers. See if they can make a balm out of it. I'm tired of being in pain All of us are."

Skye said nothing. If such a flower existed, and if anyone could find it, Adaire could. There were so many places in Faerie that had been lost for millennia.

Fiachna walked in the door, glowing with joy as Skye had never seen him. She was pleased for his happiness, and Clare's. Wished he didn't have to leave. Wished the war was over.

Wished for peace.

Once again.

But it would probably be years, perhaps decades. And she had no power to make peace happen. She just had to keep doing her part.

To forge a harmonious connection between Fae and Human.

It was all that she could do now.

She hoped it would be enough.

Her heart felt heavy with the burden of such work as well as the departure of her friends. She was now too heavy to fly.

Chapter 29 ⚜ Clare

Clare sat fully clothed in jeans and a red long sleeved T-shirt, on her unmade bed, her legs crossed beneath the blankets. Shadow and Blackheart were wrestling on the cat tower. Honey was on the perch above, occasionally slapping at the two of them, but he was really too tired to do much more than that.

The house still smelled of roast turkey and rosemary.

It was Boxing day. Fiachna had left about four in the morning. Just like he'd told her he had to.

She should have been sad or depressed.

She was, a bit. Last night had been glorious. Sex with him had been more than she had even imagined.

She'd miss him, but Clare was certain he'd return as soon as he could.

In the meantime, she had work to do.

Fall had been extraordinary at the shop. Every event brought in more people. But even better, sales were up enough that she could hire another person to help cover some of the events.

And she had come into her own. She'd begun to feel comfortable and confidant in front of crowds of people. For the first time in her life, she wasn't embarrassed to speak publicly.

It had been a long struggle to get to this place. And Clare wouldn't squander the gift, although she hadn't quite figured out how best to use it. She would get better at leading.

But today, just for today, she was going to savor the previous night and the sweetness of the kittens.

Pirate came in from the kitchen and leapt up onto the bed. She cuddled up next to Clare and began purring.

"I think you might like it here. Should we keep you here or take you back to the store when we open again? Perhaps I'll ask Skye."

She petted the black and white cat, admiring her long, soft fur.

The kittens fell off the perch, raced in circles around the bottom of it then climbed back up and stared at each other.

Clare laughed.

Her life was good.

With Fiachna it would be even better.

She'd wait.

Author's Note:

I hope you've enjoyed Book 2 of ***The Bones of the Earth Series.***

I've included two chapters of the third book – ***Faerie Descent.***

It's release will be followed closely by the remaining books.

Faerie Descent

The Bones of the Earth: Book 3

Bonus Chapters

Chapter 1 — Dylan

Dylan stood with the other water spirits in the throne room. The smoke from the fire pits made his eyes burn and his lungs ache.

Still he remained. Waiting.

Shifting his weight to the other side, glaring at Egan.

Egan sat on the magnificent golden throne, the copper braziers behind him blazing with flames. Smoke filled the room, unable to find the outlet far above. It was as if the fire Fae needed all this spectacle to prove he was good enough to be the Luminary.

That couldn't be a good sign.

The Luminary had become more scaled since Dylan had seen him last. Did that come with aging? If so, then the fire spirit had aged decades in only months. Perhaps it came from running so much power.

His forearms were covered with red, yellow and black scales as was the entire top of his head and his bare back. Egan wore golden armor over his chest and shoulders, sort of a vest. He also wore a red leathery, metallic skirt, which reminded Dylan of soldiers from ancient Rome.

Most Fae enjoyed showing off their beautiful bodies and wore no clothing or perhaps just a little something to accent a particular feature they liked about themselves. A scarf to show off their long necks. Tall gloves to show off long arms. Occasionally a transparent fabric wrapped around their bodies to add some mystery.

Egan was clearly wearing clothes as armor.

Feeling threatened?

He was talking to groups of Fae, getting their reports. Lassair, his consort, and a powerful fire spirit healer sat beside him, listening, but not speaking.

The throne room was crowded with Fae. Mostly fire spirits. They were often lizard-like and red skinned. Some had yellow or orange scales, not scaled as much as Egan though.

There were a few Earth spirits in the room and they resembled their specialty. Two millennia old tree spirits, still young, their skin not furrowed and bark-like as the elders' skin. The stone people with angular cheekbones and eyes like crystals.

The only Water spirits in the throne room were those he'd come with. Like him, they were smooth and flowing. Their softness belying their strength. Water Fae normally had pale skin, often in shades of green and blues. Although one of his companions, the elder Meredith, was quite dark of skin; she from the depths of the sea.

Missing from the throne room were the most beautiful Fae of all, the air spirits. Those glowing ethereal Fae, whose beauty made everyone gasp. Their long wavy hair often braided and beaded with gold and silver beads. Their transparent wings could fan the flames of fire Fae, cool water spirits and move fresh air to plant spirits.

They'd mostly vanished when Egan took power. In the confusion that ensued, people thought they'd simply left the court in a huff. Now, it was clear something else had happened. Something dark and sinister.

The offspring of the Fomorians were waging war on Faerie.

Who was fighting this war if there were so many gathered here?

The room had changed since he'd been here last. When he left it had been stone. Now it was formed of various metals. The copper covered walls and massive mirrored columns reflected the light and heat, making it nearly too bright and definitely too hot to bear.

Especially considering where he'd come from.

The room now held no plants, no water and the air felt so hot as to be stifling. Egan's power was out of control again.

Was it the strain of the war?

Dylan sensed the other water Fae were as uncomfortable as he was. He looked at them. Most of them were looking at the floor. Especially Kerr and Mairsile. His arms were folded in front of him, her fists clenched with fury.

The only one he knew to be calm was Meredith. Very little riled her. Yet she would be the only one of them to give Egan hell.

She stood silently, still dripping. The long, thick, silvery blue braids hanging over her teal-shaded skin, down to her knees. She was slightly hunched from many millennia of life and probably the eldest Fae in this room. There were a few others in the palace, he knew. Most of them preferred to be farther away, out in their natural element.

In the human world, Egan had spent time owning and running a successful cafe. Dylan thought the Luminary would have learned a thing or two about delegating. Making them all stand around and wait for him was unconscionable.

There was no time for this. The offspring of the Fomorians were gathering.

The heat in the metallic room made Dylan's damp skin and waist length hair dry quickly. His pale skin felt itchy from the salt drying on it and it was getting a decidedly pink tone to it. He was out of his element.

Then Egan stood and excused those he was talking to, "My friends, I must speak with the water Fae. They are drying out and miserable. And something tells me their news is pressing."

Meredith raised her head and stared into Egan's eyes.

So, she hadn't been waiting after all. She'd been sending to him, interrupting him.

The water Fae moved closed to the throne and the other Fae made room.

"We have found them," she said.

"How many are there?" asked Egan.

"Two just off the coast. Three in the deep abyss. We believe."

"You believe?" asked Egan.

"It's very difficult for us to go that deep. The water pressure is intense and painful. Even the fastest water Fae slows down to the pace of a very young child just beginning to walk. We could not survive an attack from any predator, let alone the Fomorian offspring. We cannot fight them that deep. And there isn't any cover for camouflage."

Egan nodded. "Is there enough cover for two or three of you to go down and count them. Just to see what we're up against?"

"Is the difference between three or four Fomorians worth the lives of however many Fae swim down into the Abyss? Because we would likely lose the majority of those of us who went," said Meredith, challenging him.

Egan sat up and looked at her. Reappraising the situation.

"No, I guess not. Three or four of them is more than we know how to deal with."

Meredith nodded, satisfied.

Dylan could sense the remaining liquid on the water Fae turning to steam.

He could smell hair singeing, his mouth felt dry and pasty. He would have to leave soon.

Meredith said, "You're doing it again Egan."

"What?"

"Not controlling yourself. It's far too hot in here. Take care," she said.

He looked startled, but recovered quickly, "It's not your place to criticize me."

"Well, someone has to. Do you see anyone else who has the nerve? Or who cares enough about you? Look around. Where are all the plant spirits? And the other water spirits? If you chase everyone away with your heat and anger, Faerie's demise is just around the corner."

"What makes you think the plant and water spirits aren't off on assignments?"

"Your being defensive won't help. The plant spirits aren't here because they can't tolerate your heat. The same with the water. Look at Mairsile. She's losing all her water into steam. Dylan is about to faint, but he considers you a friend so he's here," she said to Egan. "You must gain control of yourself before you can steer Faerie to a victory. We need all of us to win this war."

Meredith turned to Dylan and the others. "Shoo, all of you. Go out to the fountains. I'll be out shortly."

Dylan wanted to leave, but he had to hear Egan's reply. The others fled from the room.

Egan asked, "Is it true my friend?"

Dylan nodded, unable to speak his mouth was so dry.

"Then please leave. Go find water. Faerie is sorely depleted by the absence of our air spirits. Our home is out of balance."

"Have you found them yet?" asked Meredith.

"It seems the Fomorians have captured nearly all of them. Skye is hidden in her human body, and the elder Aura is here, afraid to leave the palace or fly. But the others… Hidden, captured or lost to us?" Egan held his hands up.

"Where do the Fomorians have them?" asked Meredith.

"I've been unable to find that out. I believe one of the winds probably has them. They're always on the move. I don't see a way out of this," said Egan.

"You must find a way," said Meredith. "What do the elders say?"

"Nonsensical things. I can't understand their thinking," he said, as if pushing away anything to do with the elders.

"Well, you will find a way. There is no alternative. We must leave you now. To rest and renew. I will return later to find out what other tasks you have for us. Think hard on the best use for us."

Meredith turned and walked out, not waiting for him to dismiss them.

Dylan followed her, the scent of his singed hair overpowering the smell of the smoky room. His eyes burned.

They moved more quickly as they got closer to the door and the cooler air in the passageway hit them. Dylan could almost breathe again without feeling like his lungs were being seared.

Once outside the palace, the temperature cooled even more. It became bearable, although still hot. They moved around to the back of the palace. There was a pool filled with fountains. Fresh water flowed into it from a stream and out towards a lake.

Dylan and Meredith joined the other water Fae there.

He slipped into the warmish water and felt his skin suck in the water, replenishing itself.

"At least his heat hasn't affected the water too much," said Meredith. She dove into the depths of the pool, completely submerging.

Everyone else joined her and they sat on the bottom of the deep end.

"*What will he do with the information you gave him?*" asked

Kerr, sending to all of their minds as it was not a private conversation.

"There is nothing he can do. Except wait them out. The Fomorians can't be reached in the Abyss. They must know that. But every day there is the opportunity for more of them to gather."

"Do you think there are more?" asked Lynette, a tone of alarm reaching her sending. "Is there something we can do?"

"I don't know if there are more. And there's nothing to do that I can think of yet, my dear," said Meredith. "The only thing that's worked against the Fomorians in the past is outsmarting them. It's time to use our minds and come up with a plan."

"There's danger down that route," said Kerr.

"Yes, there is," said Meredith, acknowledging his point that this was going behind the Luminary's back. "But the alternative is to let Faerie fall when the Fomorians attack. And they will attack. If they are able to release their imprisoned ancestors from us, then everything we've done will be lost. And we will be exterminated."

They continued to sit in the depths and talk treason.

Chapter 2 ~ Meredith

Meredith paced the gardens around the palace. Smelling the sweet pink roses and overpowering honeysuckles. The nearby world was approaching the depths of winter, but here in Faerie, summer still reigned. As it nearly always had.

Perhaps the lingering summer was due to the heat Egan exuded.

The sky above was gray. The clouds looked heavy, full of water. Rain was coming. Meredith smiled at the thought. She loved rain. The smell, the feel of water falling from the sky onto her skin. It was truly magical.

Meredith stepped off the path and entered the sacred oak grove that was nearly a thousand years old. It was dark and quiet beneath the trees. Little light came to the forest floor so there was no undergrowth.

Gathered there, seated on massive boulders in a circle were the other elders. The oldest of them all.

Alana, Brian and Ogden, all earth spirits. Alana was of the stone people, she looked as hard as a rock. Impenetrable. Brian of the hills. Tall and stately, always strong and formidable. Ogden, a dryad of the oaks. He was in his element here among these rugged trees who'd lived so long. His face was nearly as furrowed as their wrinkled bark. His hair down to his ankles, tied with leather, ornamented with strands of green moss.

Conley, a fire spirit. Nearly covered with orange and brown scales as fire elders were. His mind was keen and his actions honorable.

Lastly, there was Aura, the only remaining air spirit who'd stayed near the palace. She glowed with long life and her white hair was intricately beaded with silver beads. She wore a pale blue gauzy scarf around her waist and silver chains around her ankles and wrists. Her face beautiful, but filled with sorrow. She'd lost all the other air spirits.

Only Skye remained and she was in England. Hiding in the human body she'd made to conceal herself. Living among humans and serving as an ambassador of sorts.

"Greetings," said Meredith, bowing deeply and then sliding on top of a smooth boulder. "Thank you for coming."

"I do not know what you hope to accomplish by meeting like this," said Brian.

"I hoped we might come up with a plan to save Faerie," said Meredith.

"Why was the Luminary not invited?" asked Alana.

"Because some of us can't be around him for long," said Meredith. "He's assured me yesterday that he has no plan to deal with the offspring. If they reach the vault and release the old gods, then Faerie will be lost. Unless we can come up with a way to restrain them."

"We have been searching for such an answer since the day Egan took power," said Aura. "We have not found one."

"Meredith, you were gone from Faerie for millennia. You left when Faerie was closed. Then you returned, removed your brother from the throne and installed Egan. Now you are unhappy with the way he is leading. Why do you not simply take the throne for yourself?" asked Conley, his scales growing darker.

"Careful of the heat, Conley," said Ogden. "My trees cannot tolerate it."

Conley nodded, but continued to stare at Meredith, challenging her.

"I left when Faerie was closed, you are right. I didn't agree with the action. I didn't believe we should abandon the world to humans and their machines. I made a human body and lived among them. I don't regret my actions. I learned about humans. It was only when I was back in my own skin, swimming, that the Fomorians took me. Those Fomorians that we'd all thought were long dead. They captured many Fae, most were tortured and killed. Eight of us escaped, one of them Egan. We returned to warn Faerie that the Fomorians were still alive and killing Fae. Some of them were already here, loosening the boundaries. I had no intention of removing my brother from the throne. I hadn't even known he was Luminary before I returned. He refused to take action against the Fomorians, even though they were taking down the boundaries and invading Faerie. Egan took action. He didn't consult anyone. He simply acted to save Faerie. I used his power, and that of others, to disable the Fomorians and entomb them, alive, in the vault beneath the front courtyard of the palace. I don't regret that either. No one came forth with a better idea."

"But you did not anticipate that those same actions might wake their offspring?" asked Brian.

"I didn't even know their offspring were still alive. Since the Fomorians had mated with Fae, I'd assumed their offspring were mortal, like us. That they'd died over the long ages. What I do know is that the old gods offspring are formidable. They have qualities from the best of both lines. Perhaps not as strong as the Fomorians, but they're more crafty in the ways of the world. We are lucky they don't know how to use human technology."

"You have spent too much time among humans," said Conley.

"And you, too little."

"You have cleverly avoided addressing Conley's accusation about wanting the throne," said Alana.

"I have no desire to be Luminary. I would not be skilled as a leader for all Fae. I have far too little patience and wisdom. I believe the Luminary must be young enough to be willing to work with the humans. Their numbers are vast. We cannot afford to ignore them and their foolish destruction of this world that we all share."

Her words seemed to satisfy Conley.

"I just want to save Faerie," said Meredith. "And I fear we don't have much time. The longer we wait to act, the more time it gives the Fomorians to gather and attack us."

"At least we would get them all if we wait," said Aura.

"We have no guarantee of that. They might attack in waves," said Brian.

"Do you have a plan?" asked Alana.

Rain began to fall. Some of it dropped between the leaves, wetting her just a bit. The air freshened. She noticed the rain hitting Conley evaporated almost immediately with a hissing sound.

Meredith held out her hand catching a few drops and watching her skin absorb the water. She was still too dried out from being near Egan.

"No," said Meredith. "If I did have a plan, I would act. All that I know is that in the old stories, the Fomorians were originally defeated by letting them become us. We lived side by side with them for a very long time. Those that didn't wither and sleep were assimilated by intermarriage with us. Then, millennia later we thought them all dead and they arose again. Egan took power and we captured them by using our wits. We aren't as strong as they are. We can't out muscle them. Which is what Egan is trying to do now."

They nodded.

"I agree, we must use our minds," said Alana.

"I believe the elders carry the wisdom of Faerie. We are the ones who will come up with a solution. But we must do it quickly," said Meredith.

"I still think Egan should be a part of this," said Conley.

"He is too busy," said Alana. "He is running a war."

"I agree, he should be included," said Brian.

"I cannot bear his heat," said Ogden.

Meredith said, "I cannot either, not for long."

Aura said, "I think he should be part of this as well. I am not strong enough to mitigate his heat for the two of you. The loss of being able to fly and the absence of my kind has left me weak."

"Do we need to bring Skye back to help you?" asked Meredith.

"No. She is safer hiding among humans. And she is performing a valuable service. We may need the humans in all of this."

"What do you mean need the humans?" asked Alana.

"I think they may have a part to play in this war. This negotiation with the offspring. I cannot see if yet though, perhaps it is just a feeling," said Aura, fluttering her transparent wings.

Meredith hadn't considered that.

She'd simply thought that humans and Fae needed to work out an arrangement. And that Faerie needed to guide humans' development, to put a limit on their expansion in the natural world.

"I do not see humans having a part of any of this," said Ogden.

They talked for a time, not coming to any agreement, but they were talking at least. None of them would go up against Egan. Some of them might even inform him she was talking treason.

Egan was a powerful Fae and Luminaries in the past had been quick to punish Fae who caused dissension, sometimes even killing them.

But this wasn't treason, not to Meredith.

Not when the Luminary was unfit to rule. The problem was, there was no other contender. No other Fae who had the necessary skills to fight the Fomorians.

Hours later, they left. One by one. At least deciding to consider the question and to meet again tomorrow.

Meredith continued on the path down to the lake. She dove in, swimming through the rushes, scattering schools of small fish.

The water was colder here. Murky from the mud at the bottom, but her eyes adjusted. She reveled in the cool wetness.

Meredith found the center of the lake and floated there, far below the surface, barely moving. She felt other water spirits and fish join her. Giving support as she pondered the questions brought up in the meeting.

What role could humans have in this war? She didn't hold out much hope that technology could conquer the Fomorians' offspring. Humans always put great store in their inventions. But how does one subdue the wind, or the sea?

She had no answers. But that didn't mean it was time to stop looking.

About the Author

Linda Jordan writes fascinating characters, funny dialogue, and imaginative fiction. She creates both long and short fiction, serious and silly. She believes in the power of healing and transformation, and many of her stories follow those themes.

In a previous lifetime, Linda coordinated the Clarion West Writers' Workshop as well as the Reading Series. She spent four years as Chair of the Board of Directors during Clarion West's formative period. She's also worked as a travel agent, a baker, and a pond plant/fish sales person, you know, the sort of things one does as a writer.

Linda now lives in the rainy wilds of Washington state with her husband, daughter, four cats, eighteen Koi and an infinite number of slugs and snails.

Visit her at: www.LindaJordan.net

Metamorphosis Press website is at: www.MetamorphosisPress.com

If you enjoyed this story, please consider leaving a review at Goodreads or your favorite online retailer to help like-minded readers discover it. Thank you!

Get a FREE ebook!
Sign up for Linda's Serendipitous Newsletter at her website: www.LindaJordan.net

Made in the USA
San Bernardino, CA
04 April 2018